Bruce Wayne

Participation Award recipient and distinguished gentleman

DC COMICS
SECRET HERO SOCIETY

DETENTION OF DOOM

Written by **Derek Fridolfs** | Illustrations by **Dustin Nguyen**

SCHOLASTIC INC.

To all my wonderful teachers and educators throughout the years at McCardle Elementary, Ahwahnee Middle School, and Hoover High School, allowing for my mind to wander, be inspired, and get creative. And still I managed to stay out of detention! — Derek

Thank you to my wife, Nicole, for the love, support, and taking care of real-life things so that I can live in the imaginary. My kids, Bradley and Kaeli, for keeping me always inspired and forever excited about the things to come. — Dustin

ALL RIGHTS RESERVED. PUBLISHED BY SCHOLASTIC INC., *PUBLISHERS SINCE 1920.* SCHOLASTIC AND ASSOCIATED LOGOS ARE TRADEMARKS AND/OR REGISTERED TRADEMARKS OF SCHOLASTIC INC.

THE PUBLISHER DOES NOT HAVE ANY CONTROL OVER AND DOES NOT ASSUME ANY RESPONSIBILITY FOR AUTHOR OR THIRD-PARTY WEBSITES OR THEIR CONTENT.

THIS BOOK IS A WORK OF FICTION. NAMES, CHARACTERS, PLACES, AND INCIDENTS ARE EITHER THE PRODUCT OF THE AUTHOR'S IMAGINATION OR ARE USED FICTITIOUSLY, AND ANY RESEMBLANCE TO ACTUAL PERSONS, LIVING OR DEAD, BUSINESS ESTABLISHMENTS, EVENTS, OR LOCALES IS ENTIRELY COINCIDENTAL.

ISBN 978-1-338-03312-0

10 9 8 7 6 5 4 3 2 1   18 19 20 21 22

PRINTED IN THE U.S.A.   23
FIRST PRINTING 2018

BOOK DESIGN BY RICK DEMONICO AND CHEUNG TAI

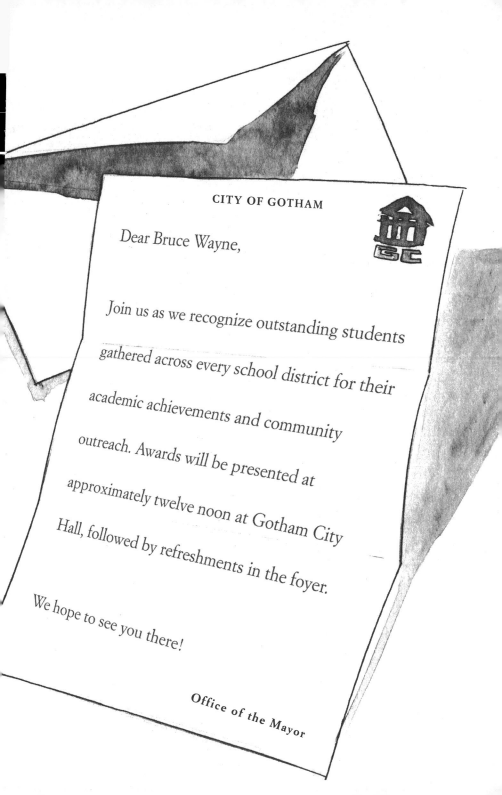

CITY OF GOTHAM

Dear Bruce Wayne,

Join us as we recognize outstanding students gathered across every school district for their academic achievements and community outreach. Awards will be presented at approximately twelve noon at Gotham City Hall, followed by refreshments in the foyer.

We hope to see you there!

Office of the Mayor

WELCOME, STUDENTS
WHAT A SPLENDID TURNOUT!
I DON'T EVEN KNOW WHY I'M HERE.
THE AWARD FOR BRAVERY GOES TO CLARK KENT, FOR HIS EFFORTS TO RESCUE A BUS FULL OF CHILDREN AT AN ACCIDENT IN SMALLVILLE.
THE PEACE PRIZE HAS BEEN AWARDED TO MISS DIANA PRINCE, FOR HIGH ACADEMIC ACHIEVEMENT AS A MODEL TRANSFER STUDENT.

THE NEXT AWARD GOES TO . . .
. . . BRUCE WAYNE.
THAT WOULD BE YOU, SIR.
WHAT'S THIS AWARD FOR?
AH, YES . . . THE PARTICIPATION AWARD.
WHEN DID YOU EVER "PARTICIPATE"?
APPARENTLY TODAY, BY BEING HERE.

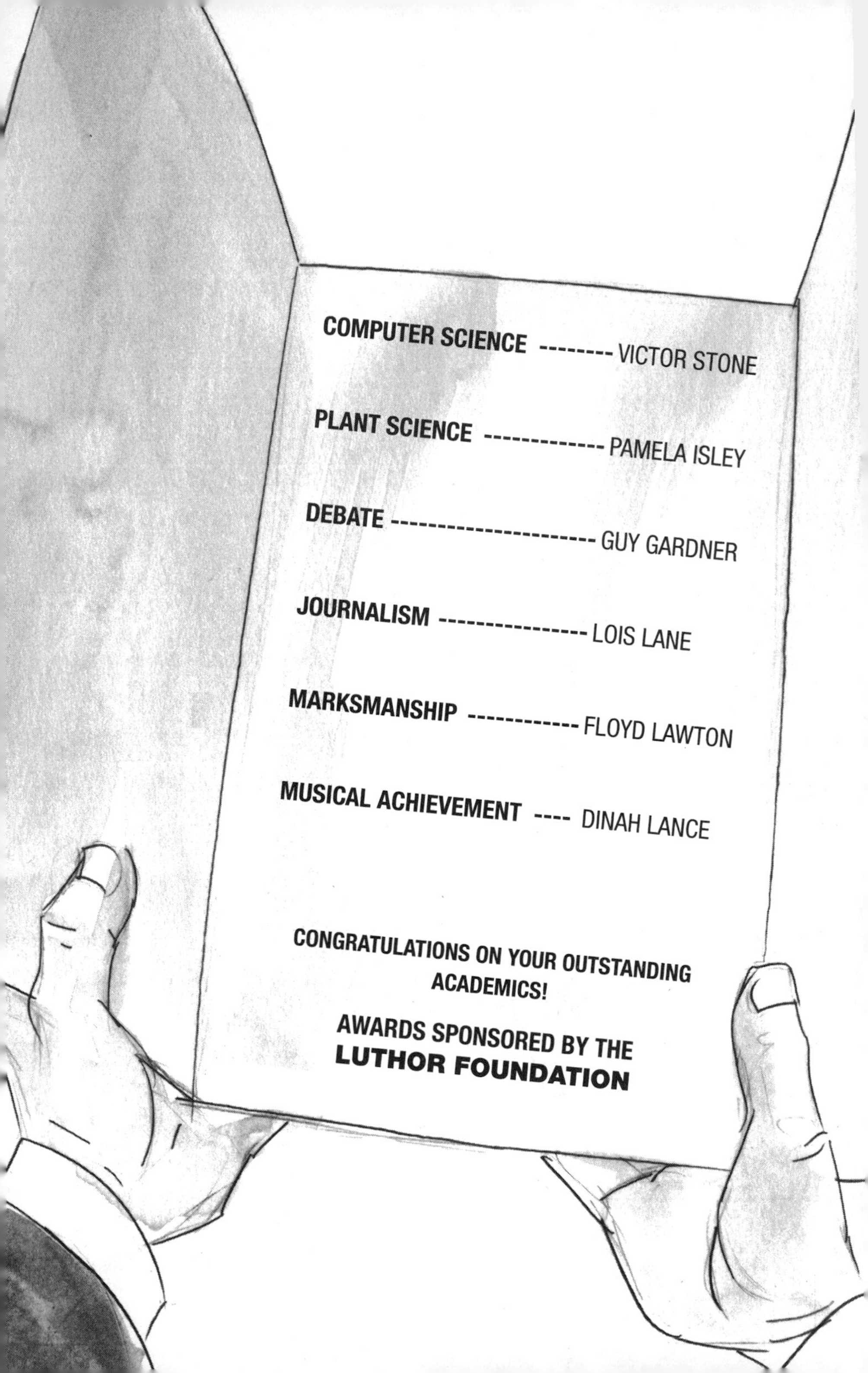

COMPUTER SCIENCE -------- VICTOR STONE

PLANT SCIENCE ------------ PAMELA ISLEY

DEBATE -------------------- GUY GARDNER

JOURNALISM --------------- LOIS LANE

MARKSMANSHIP ------------ FLOYD LAWTON

MUSICAL ACHIEVEMENT ---- DINAH LANCE

CONGRATULATIONS ON YOUR OUTSTANDING
ACADEMICS!

AWARDS SPONSORED BY THE
LUTHOR FOUNDATION

CONGRATULATIONS

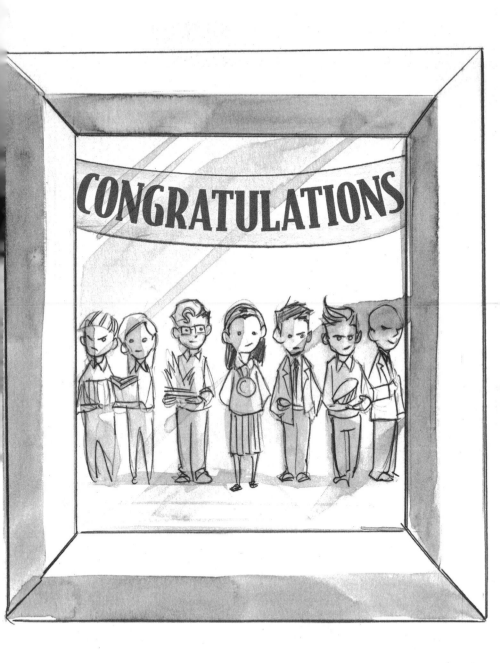

I AM SO PROUD OF ALL OF YOU. MASTER BRUCE AND I WOULD LIKE TO INVITE YOU BACK FOR LUNCH.
THANK YOU, MR. PENNYWORTH.
THAT'S A VERY NICE TROPHY, CLARK. EVEN BETTER THAN BRUCE'S.
ONE DAY, MY TROPHY ROOM WILL BE FILLED WITH COOL THINGS.
I CAN'T WAIT TO SHOW IT TO MA AND PA!
FRIZZAP
WHOA!

WHERE DID MASTER CLARK DISAPPEAR TO?
THAT'S WHAT I WANT TO KNOW!
WHAT BRUCE MEANT TO SAY IS, CLARK HAD TO LEAVE UNEXPECTEDLY.
WE SHOULD GO ASK LEX. MAYBE HE'LL KNOW WHY.
LUNCH FOR ONE, THEN.

PRIVATE SCHOOL
DAILY PLANET
Diana,
check out Lex's private school he attends. He should be there.
I'll go check out the newspaper for any leads.

MESSAGES

GROUP CHAT

hows your search turning out?

It's not

?

Lex's school won't let me on campus

did you get caught sneaking in?

no I just walked in the front

why did you do that?

you need to be more stealthy and sneaky like me

not everyone is you

tell me about it!

maybe I can help

Hey Vic!

ok I've reprogrammed your records to make you a student there Diana

booyah ez access!

Thanks Vic!

no prob

Bruce I've also sent you some other locations Lex likes to hang out

most of these say INTERGANG

SEND

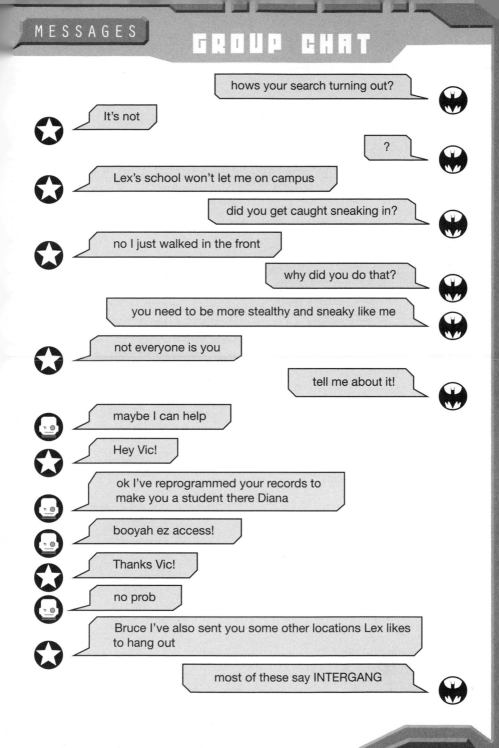

GROUP CHAT

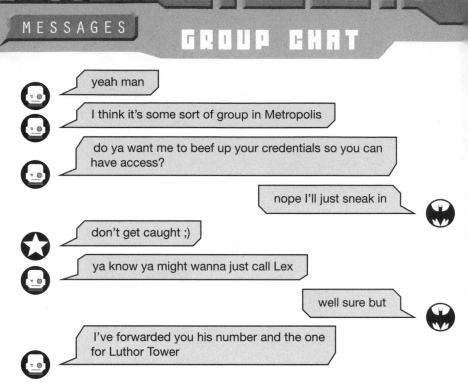

yeah man

I think it's some sort of group in Metropolis

do ya want me to beef up your credentials so you can have access?

nope I'll just sneak in

don't get caught ;)

ya know ya might wanna just call Lex

well sure but

I've forwarded you his number and the one for Luthor Tower

< USER HAS LOGGED OFF >

SEND

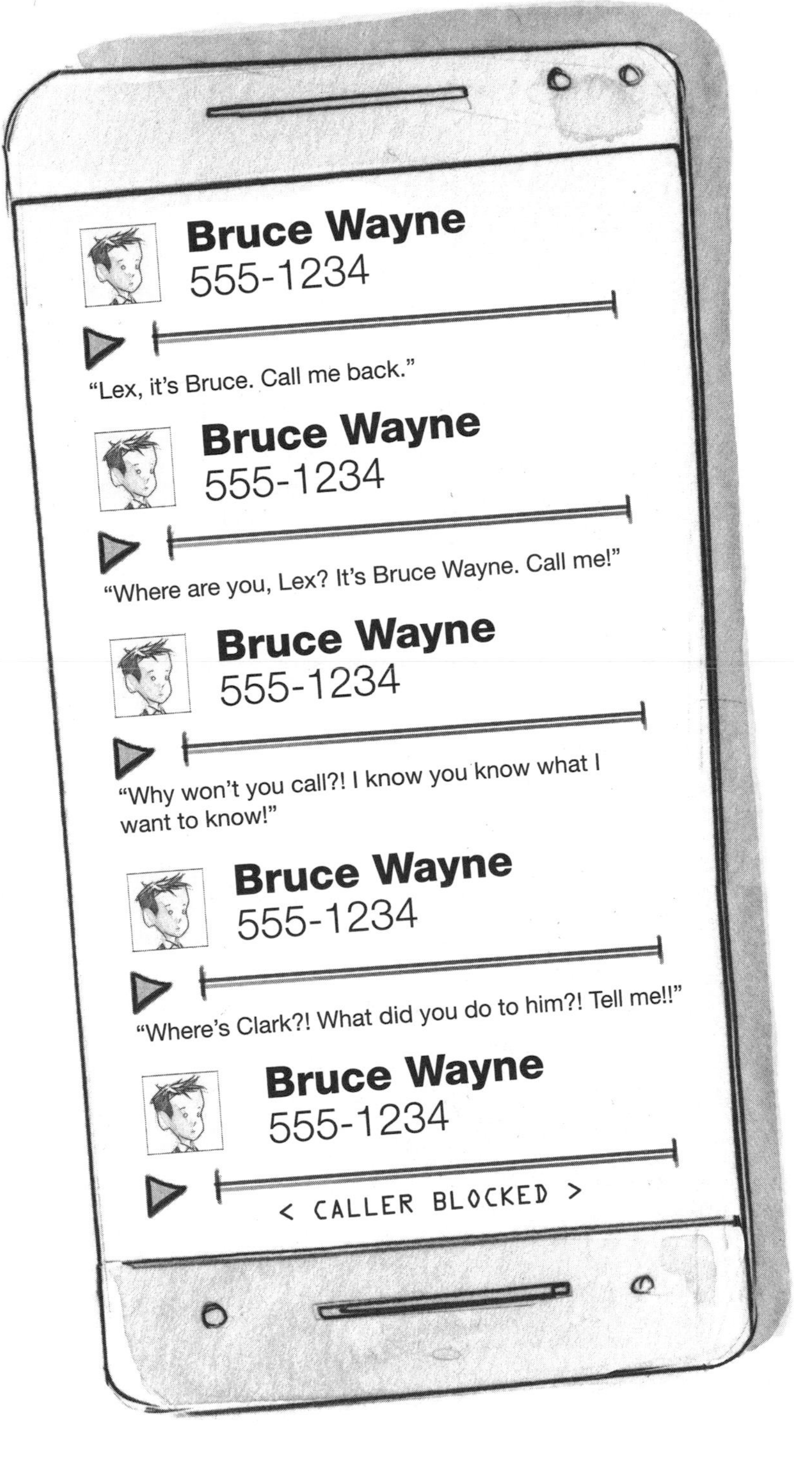
Bruce Wayne
555-1234
"Lex, it's Bruce. Call me back."
Bruce Wayne
555-1234
"Where are you, Lex? It's Bruce Wayne. Call me!"
Bruce Wayne
555-1234
"Why won't you call?! I know you know what I want to know!"
Bruce Wayne
555-1234
"Where's Clark?! What did you do to him?! Tell me!!"
Bruce Wayne
555-1234
< CALLER BLOCKED >

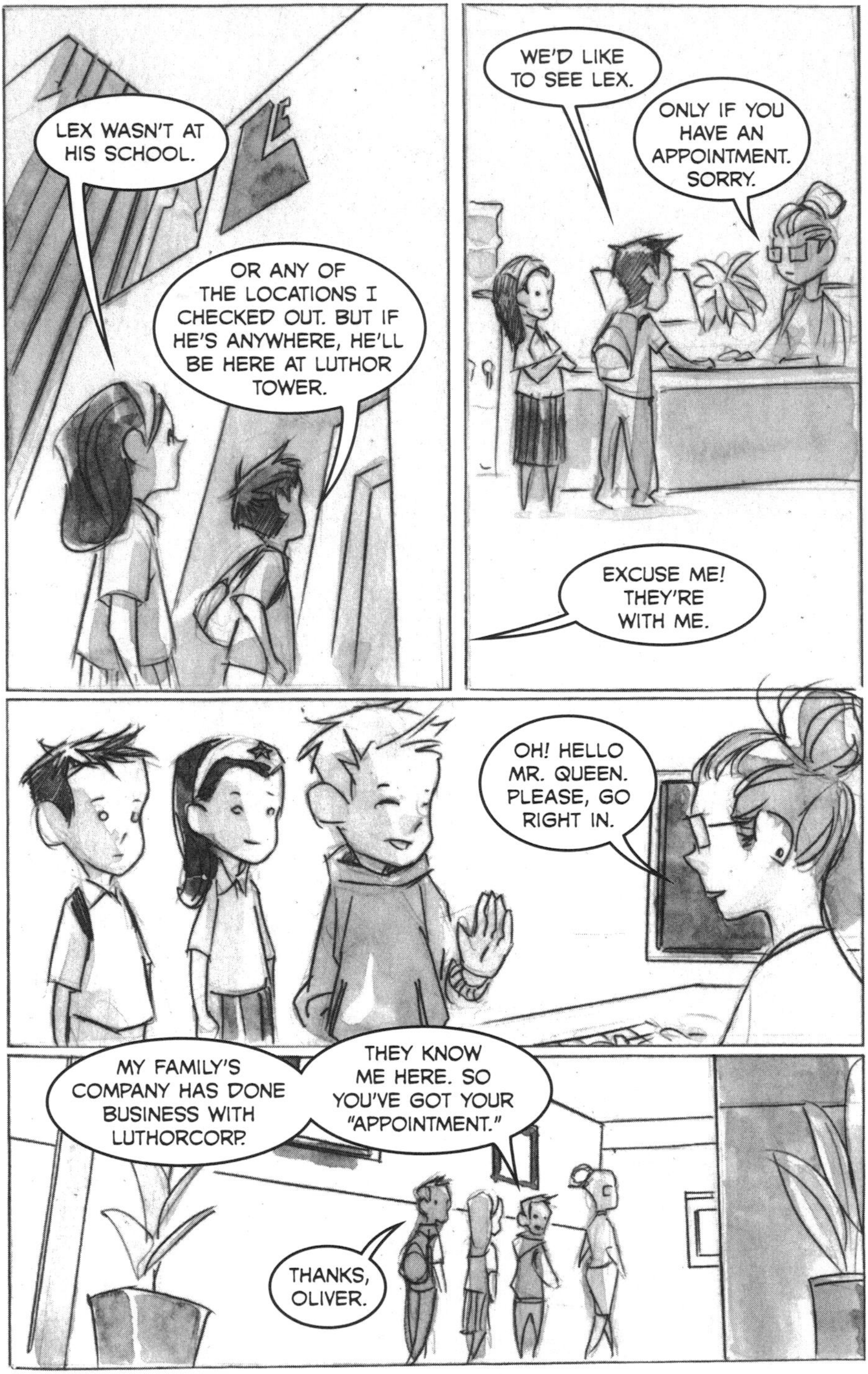
LEX WASN'T AT HIS SCHOOL.
OR ANY OF THE LOCATIONS I CHECKED OUT. BUT IF HE'S ANYWHERE, HE'LL BE HERE AT LUTHOR TOWER.
WE'D LIKE TO SEE LEX.
ONLY IF YOU HAVE AN APPOINTMENT. SORRY.
EXCUSE ME! THEY'RE WITH ME.
OH! HELLO MR. QUEEN. PLEASE, GO RIGHT IN.
MY FAMILY'S COMPANY HAS DONE BUSINESS WITH LUTHORCORP.
THEY KNOW ME HERE. SO YOU'VE GOT YOUR "APPOINTMENT."
THANKS, OLIVER.

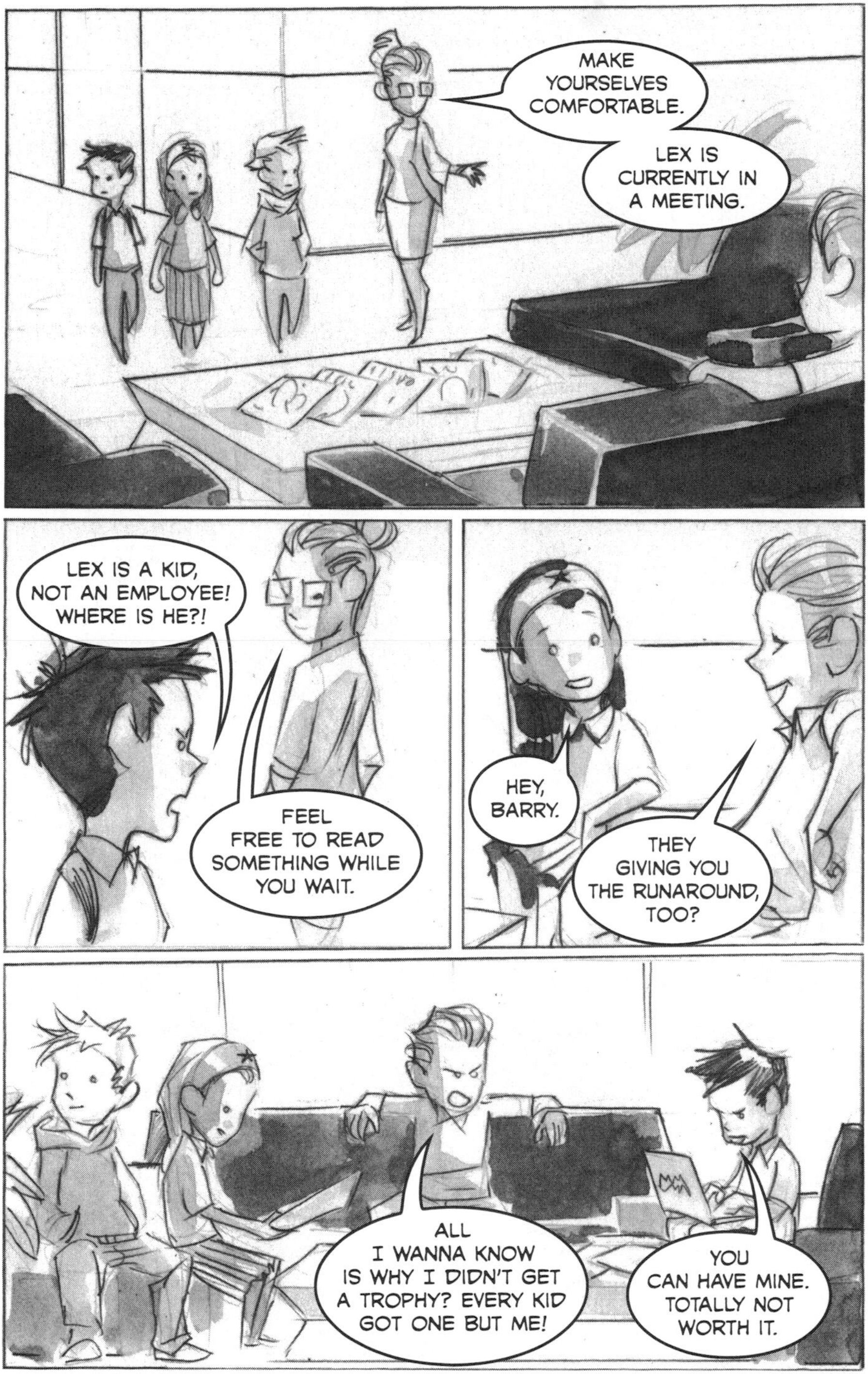
MAKE YOURSELVES COMFORTABLE.
LEX IS CURRENTLY IN A MEETING.
LEX IS A KID, NOT AN EMPLOYEE! WHERE IS HE?!
FEEL FREE TO READ SOMETHING WHILE YOU WAIT.
HEY, BARRY.
THEY GIVING YOU THE RUNAROUND, TOO?
ALL I WANNA KNOW IS WHY I DIDN'T GET A TROPHY? EVERY KID GOT ONE BUT ME!
YOU CAN HAVE MINE. TOTALLY NOT WORTH IT.

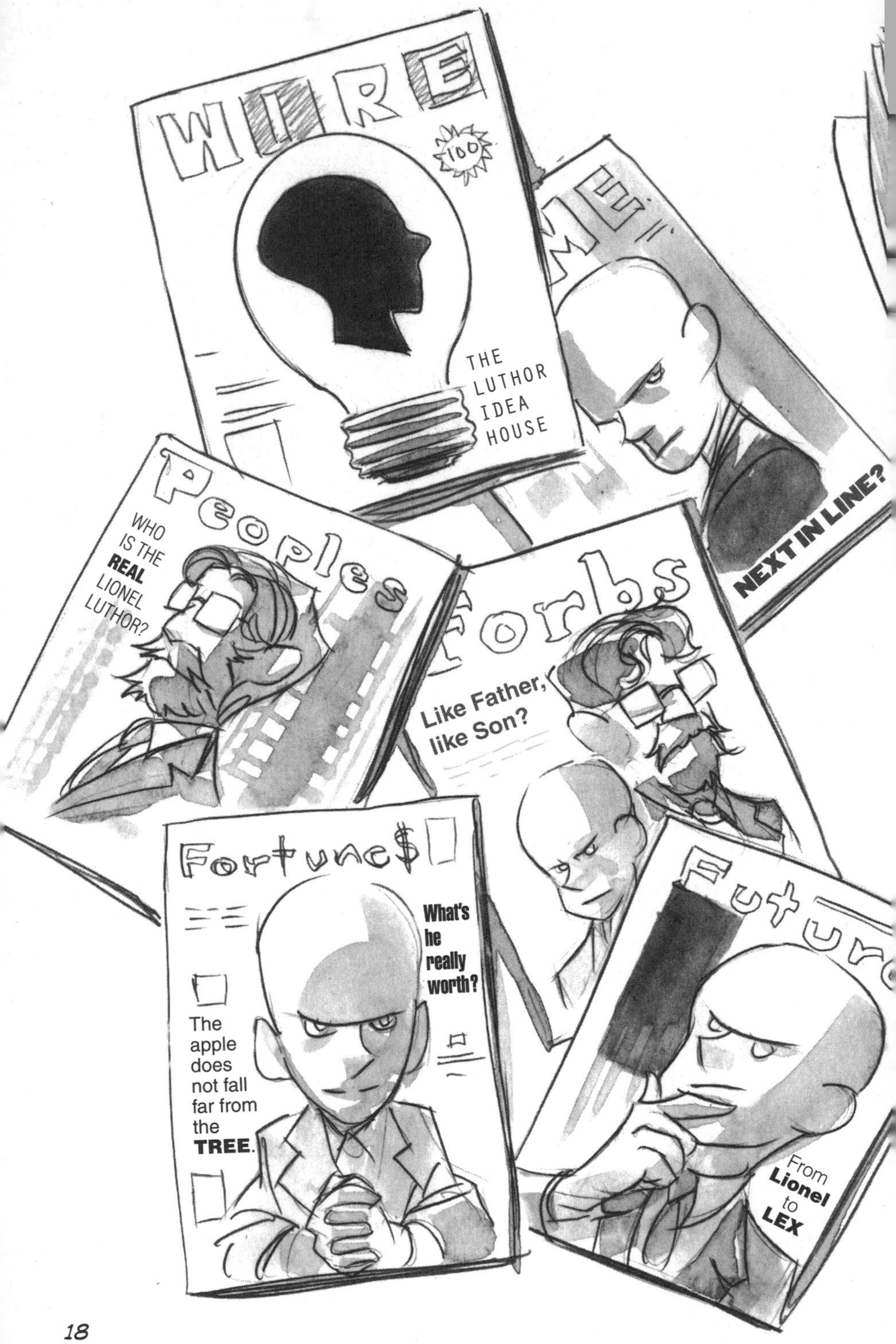
WIRE
100
THE LUTHOR IDEA HOUSE
NEXT IN LINE?
Peoples
WHO IS THE REAL LIONEL LUTHOR?
Forbs
Like Father, like Son?
Fortune$
What's he really worth?
The apple does not fall far from the TREE.
Futur
From Lionel to LEX

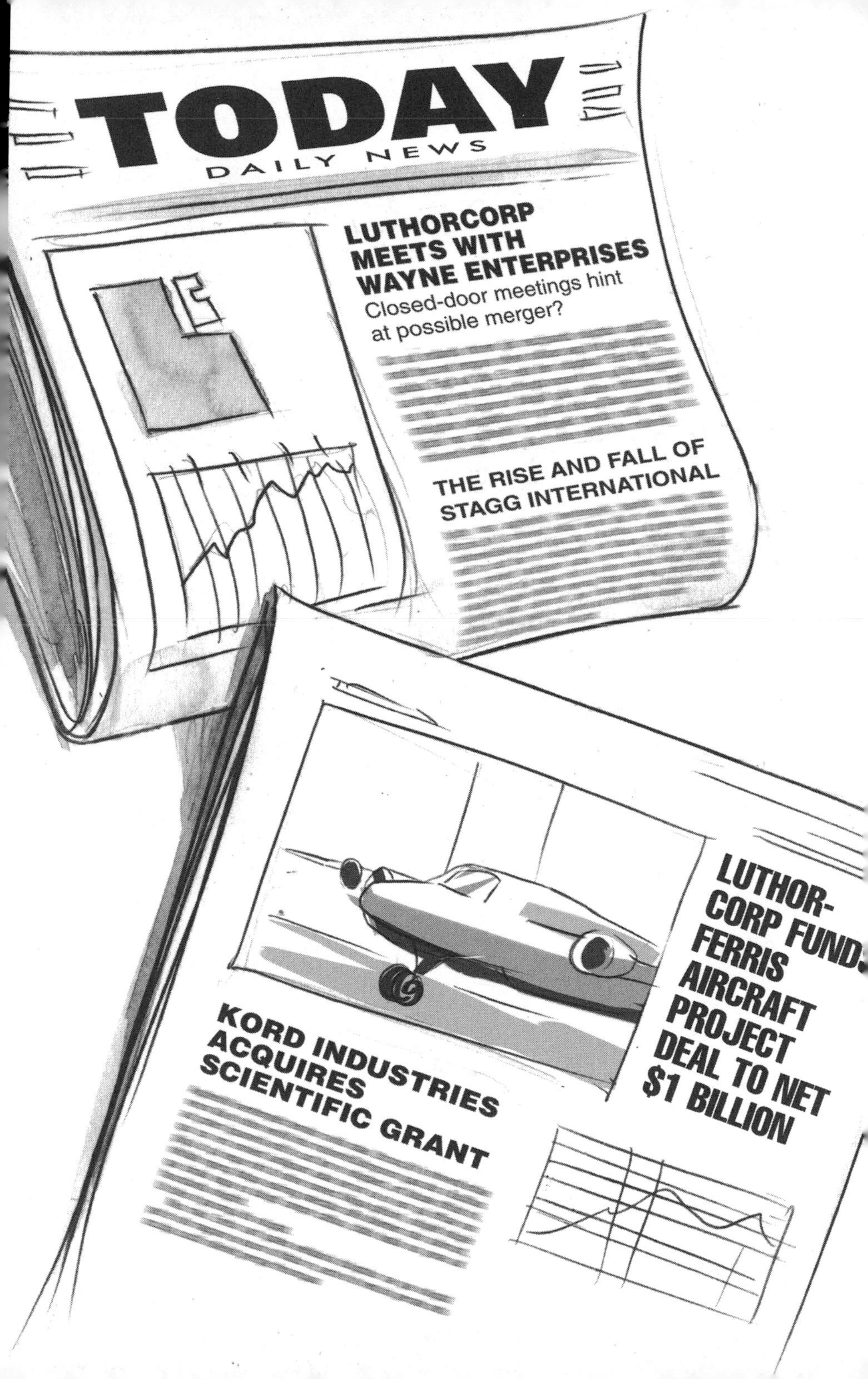
TODAY
DAILY NEWS
LUTHORCORP MEETS WITH WAYNE ENTERPRISES
Closed-door meetings hint at possible merger?
THE RISE AND FALL OF STAGG INTERNATIONAL
LUTHOR-CORP FUNDS FERRIS AIRCRAFT PROJECT DEAL TO NET $1 BILLION
KORD INDUSTRIES ACQUIRES SCIENTIFIC GRANT

MESSAGES

GROUP CHAT

Vic are you there?

Always! I'm playing Smash City Saviors with the new DLC character and

sorry to interrupt but I need your help

Still having trouble at Luthor Tower?

right

I need a distraction

not for me but for the receptionist

so I can go do my thing without being watched

can you provide that?

One computer server meltdown coming right up!

SEND

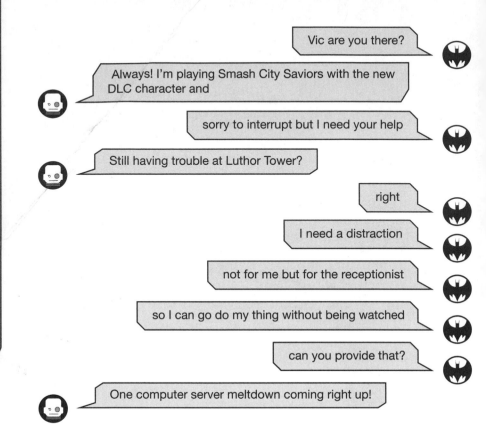

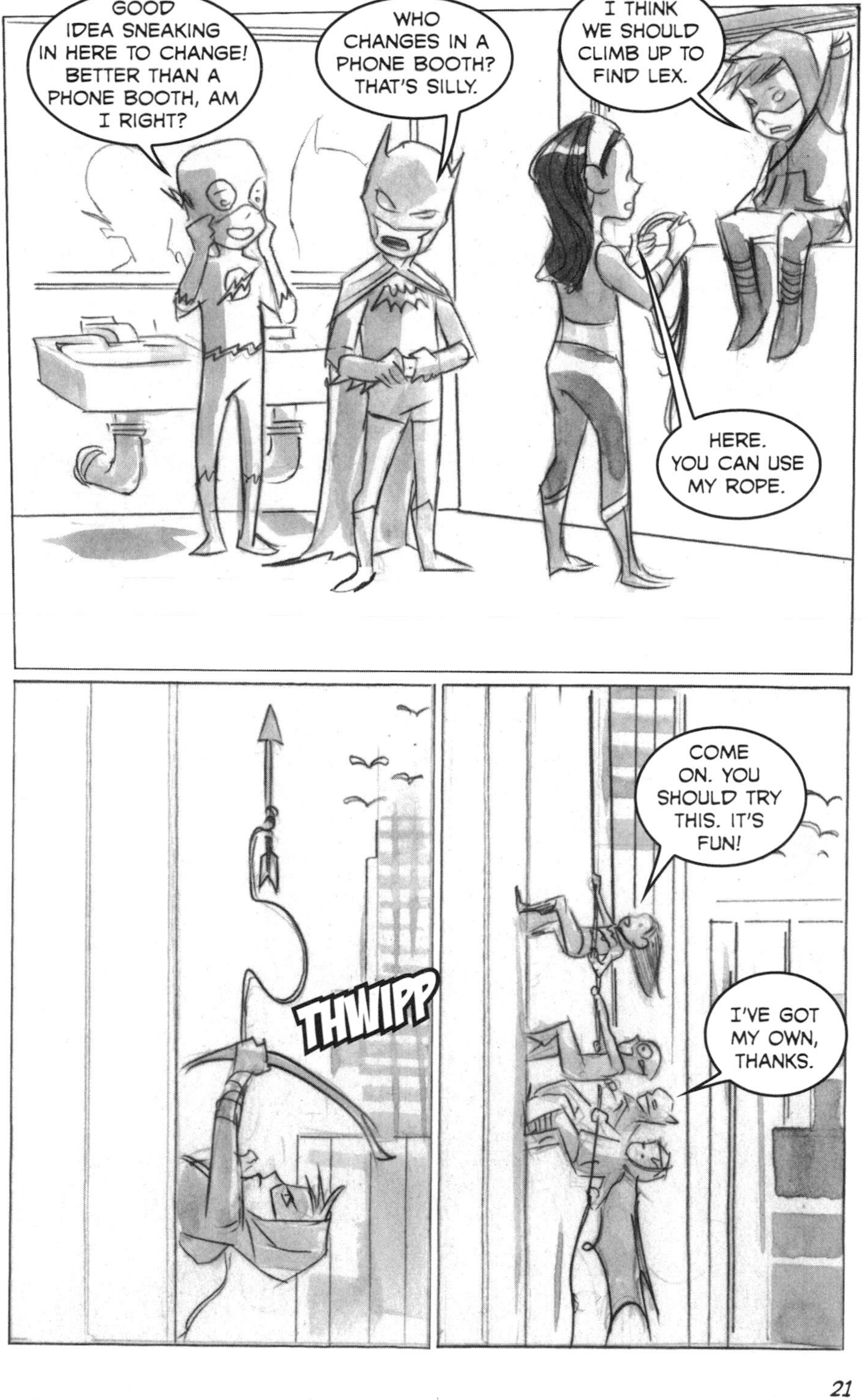
GOOD IDEA SNEAKING IN HERE TO CHANGE! BETTER THAN A PHONE BOOTH, AM I RIGHT?
WHO CHANGES IN A PHONE BOOTH? THAT'S SILLY.
I THINK WE SHOULD CLIMB UP TO FIND LEX.
HERE. YOU CAN USE MY ROPE.
THWIPP
COME ON. YOU SHOULD TRY THIS. IT'S FUN!
I'VE GOT MY OWN, THANKS.

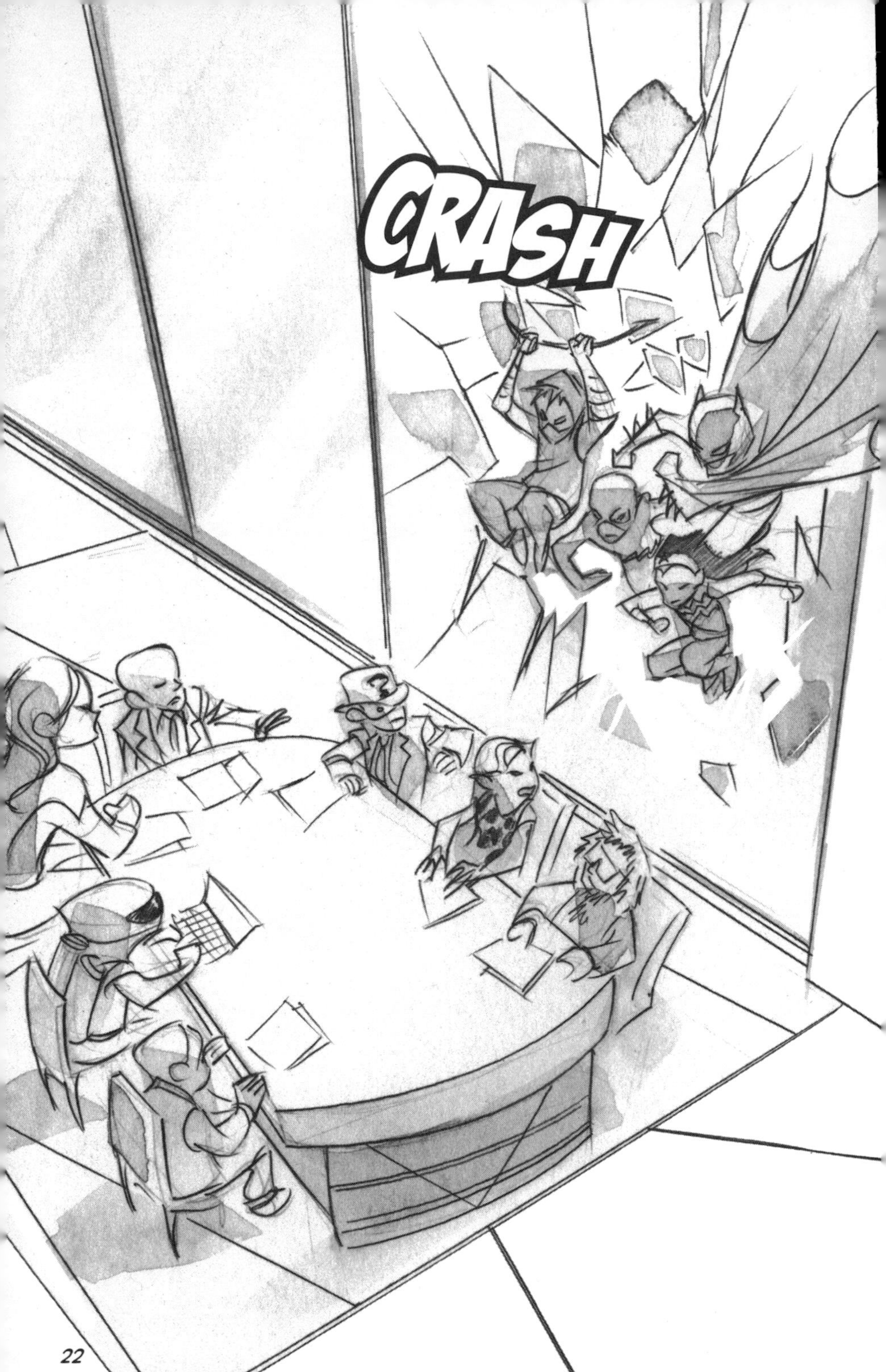
CRASH

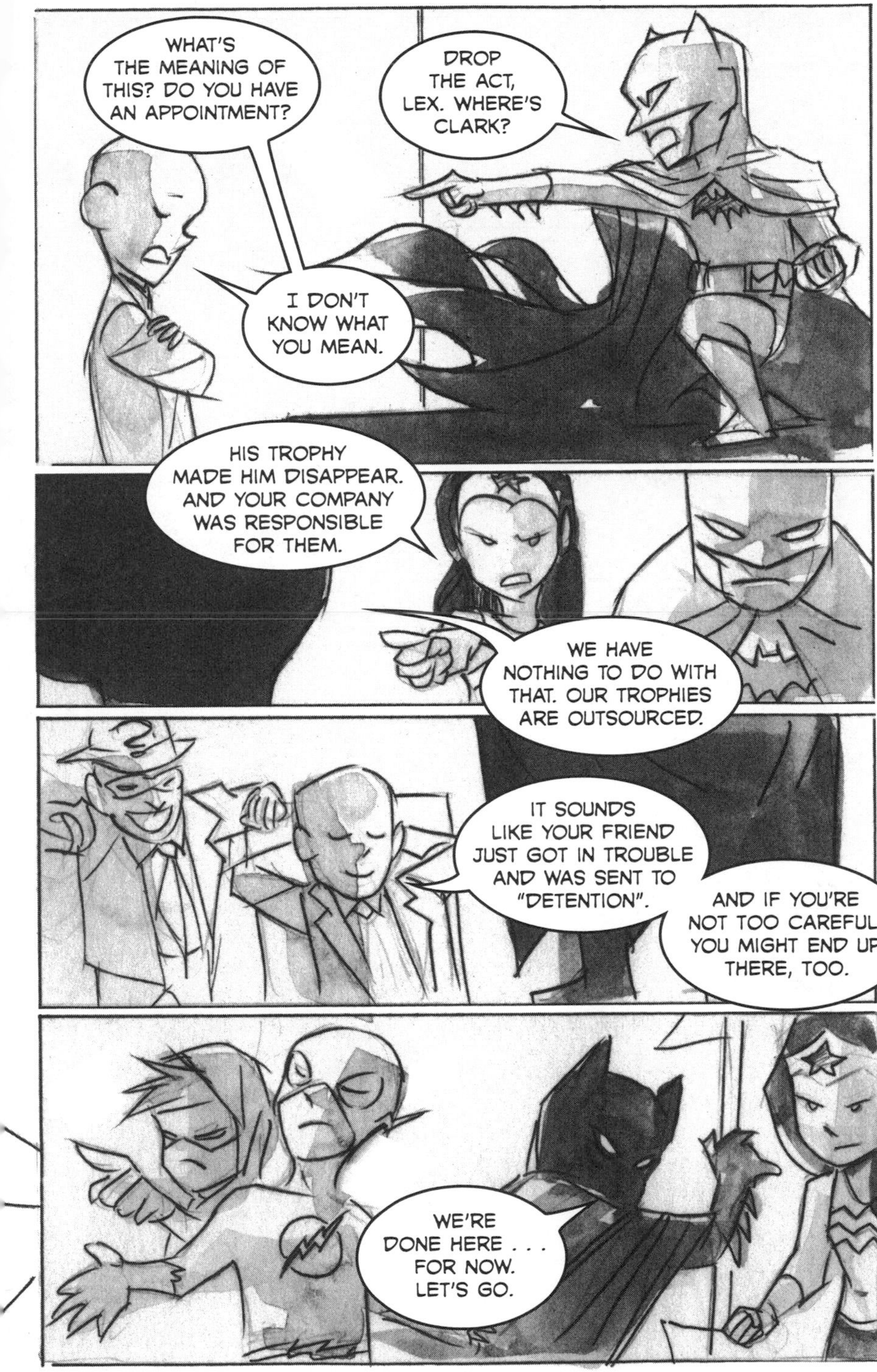
WHAT'S THE MEANING OF THIS? DO YOU HAVE AN APPOINTMENT?
DROP THE ACT, LEX. WHERE'S CLARK?
I DON'T KNOW WHAT YOU MEAN.
HIS TROPHY MADE HIM DISAPPEAR. AND YOUR COMPANY WAS RESPONSIBLE FOR THEM.
WE HAVE NOTHING TO DO WITH THAT. OUR TROPHIES ARE OUTSOURCED.
IT SOUNDS LIKE YOUR FRIEND JUST GOT IN TROUBLE AND WAS SENT TO "DETENTION".
AND IF YOU'RE NOT TOO CAREFUL, YOU MIGHT END UP THERE, TOO.
WE'RE DONE HERE . . . FOR NOW. LET'S GO.

MESSAGES

GROUP CHAT

Vic you still there?

What do you need now?

Clark is missing and I need your help to find him

I've tapped into some satellites to search

it's coming up empty

nothing in Smallville, Metropolis, Gotham City, or even Earth

Lex has something to do with this I'm sure of it

can you run a background check on LuthorCorp?

they are the ones responsible for giving out some suspicious trophies

on it!

. . .

nothing here either

but this is weird

what?

SEND

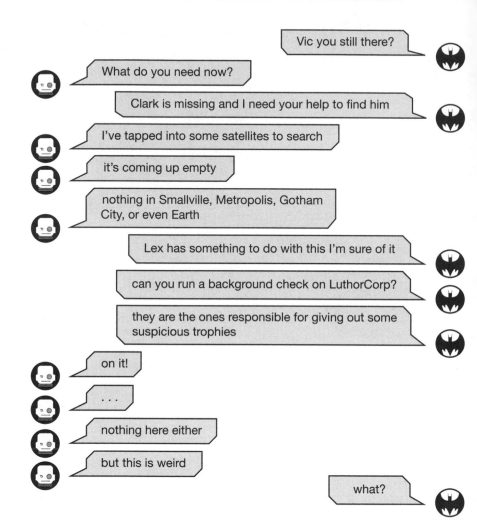

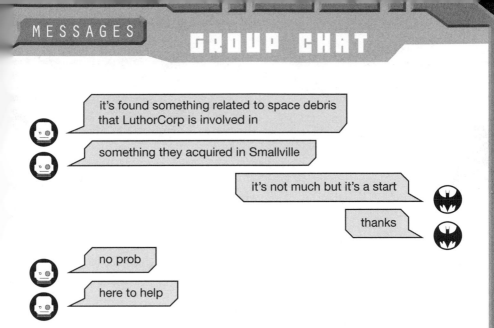

it's found something related to space debris that LuthorCorp is involved in

something they acquired in Smallville

it's not much but it's a start

thanks

no prob

here to help

SEND

USERNAME: BWAYNE
RE: JOURNAL ENTRY 1

CLARK REMAINS MISSING, NO DOUBT THANKS TO LEX. THAT KID HAS HAD IT IN FOR CLARK EVER SINCE THEY RAN AGAINST EACH OTHER FOR SCHOOL PRESIDENT. ONE MINUTE, CLARK IS AT MY HOME CHECKING OUT HIS TROPHY. THE NEXT MINUTE, THE TROPHY MADE HIM DISAPPEAR! IT MAKES ME HATE TROPHIES EVEN MORE NOW.

SOME FRIENDS AND I WENT TO TRACK DOWN LEX TO GET TO THE BOTTOM OF IT, BUT LEX WAS NO HELP. HE'S NOT VERY GOOD AT PLAYING COY, AS I CAN TELL, HE WAS JUST LYING WHENEVER WE ASKED HIM FOR HIS HELP. LUTHORCORP WAS RESPONSIBLE FOR OFFERING THE SCHOOL TROPHIES, BUT WE'VE COME UP EMPTY FINDING OUT WHY OR HOW THEY'RE INVOLVED.

BUT NOW VIC HAS OFFERED SOME INFORMATION PERTAINING TO LUTHORCORP IN SMALLVILLE, WHICH IS CLARK'S HOMETOWN. IT'S WORTH CHECKING INTO. IT'S LUCKY I STILL HAVE ACCESS TO MY ALLOWANCE. BECAUSE I'M GOING TO NEED IT TO ORDER SOME BUS TICKETS ONLINE FOR DIANA AND ME TO GO CHECK THINGS OUT. BARRY'S ON HIS OWN. THAT KID CAN RUN THERE! BESIDES, I WON'T HAVE TO HEAR HIM CONSTANTLY TALKING AND BEING ANNOYING.

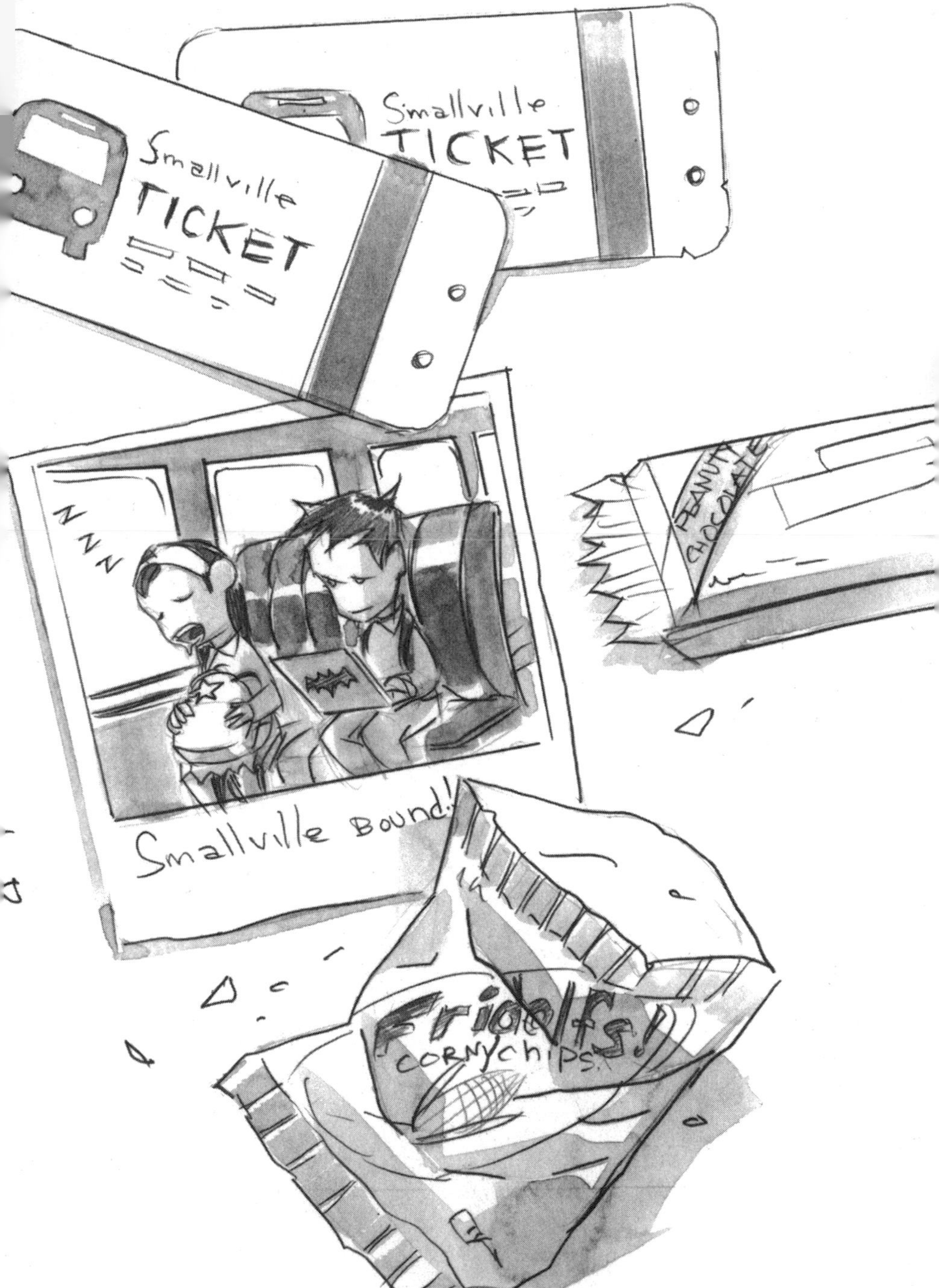
Smallville
TICKET
Smallville
TICKET
NNN
Smallville Bound!
PEANUTY
CHOCOLATE
CORNYCHIPS

it's taking you guys forever

are you already there Barry?

yeah like hours ago

buses are for losers

I've already run across Smallville and checked the whole town out

lots of farms and cows

mooooooooo

Barry!

why would Clark want to live here?

Smallville

more like Dullsville

SEND

MESSAGES

GROUP CHAT

that's not nice Barry

got nothing else to do while I wait for you slowpokes

just sitting at this malt shop

and trying everything on the menu

check it out

BARRY!

when are you gonna get here?

are you here yet?

are you here yet?

are you here yet?

< USER BLOCKED >

what happened?

we'll talk to him when we get there

SEND

FROM: PENNY_1
TO: BWAYNE
SUBJECT: WHERE ARE YOU?

MASTER BRUCE,

WHEN YOU INVITE FRIENDS OVER FOR LUNCH, IT IS
RESPONSIBLE OF THE HOST TO ACTUALLY REMAIN FOR IT.
YOU DIDN'T EVEN LEAVE A FORWARDING NOTE REGARDING
WHERE YOU AND YOUR FRIENDS TOOK OFF TO.

SINCE YOU ARE NOT ANSWERING YOUR TEXTS, I HOPE YOU
RECEIVE THIS EMAIL AND CALL TO LET ME KNOW YOUR
LOCATION. I REGRET TO INFORM YOU THAT YOUR LUNCH IS
NOW COLD AND EATEN. DON'T LET YOUR DINNER SUFFER THE
SAME FATE.

SINCERELY,

ALFRED

Smallville Gazette

S.T.A.
LAB

THE SKY IS FALLING
Asteroids Descend on Smallville

Local farmers put their crops and families to bed overnight, only to wake up the next morning to an invasion. "I heard the sound of something hitting the barn. And when I checked the fields, there were craters," said Theodore MacDonald. "It's like nothing I ever seen!"

All reports and eyewitness accounts seem to point to a meteor shower that rained down over Smallville, leaving miles of rocky debris along roads and fields. The damage is still being calculated.

"Meteors falling through our atmosphere is very common," said a spokesperson from S.T.A.R. Labs, located in Metropolis. "But most disintegrate upon entry into Earth's atmosphere. It's rare for so many meteorites to remain intact."

Story continued on page A7

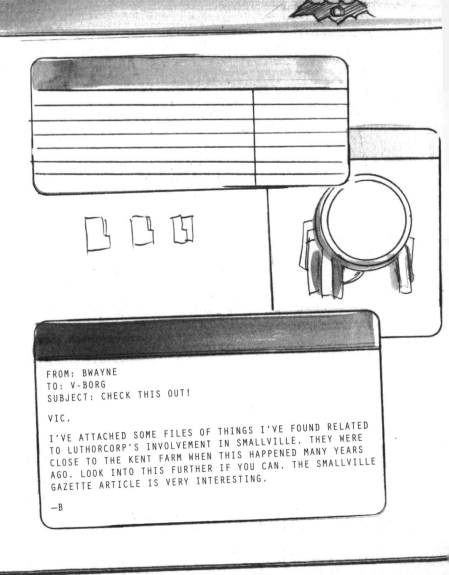

FROM: BWAYNE
TO: V-BORG
SUBJECT: CHECK THIS OUT!

VIC,

I'VE ATTACHED SOME FILES OF THINGS I'VE FOUND RELATED
TO LUTHORCORP'S INVOLVEMENT IN SMALLVILLE. THEY WERE
CLOSE TO THE KENT FARM WHEN THIS HAPPENED MANY YEARS
AGO. LOOK INTO THIS FURTHER IF YOU CAN. THE SMALLVILLE
GAZETTE ARTICLE IS VERY INTERESTING.

—B

MONITOR 01
14:10:08
MONITOR 02
14:10:32
MONITOR 03
14:11:15
MONITOR 04
< CAM FOOTAGE >
< DELETE ALL >
14:11:38

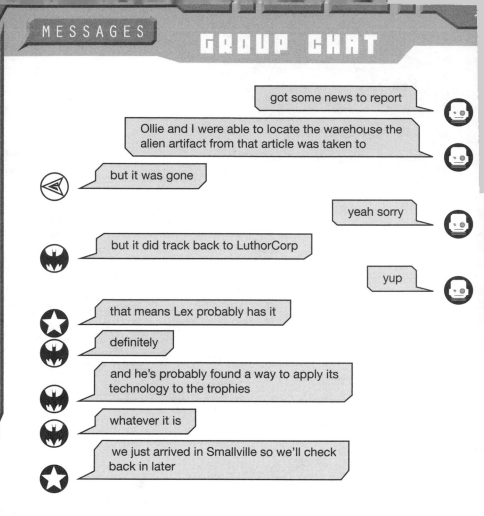

got some news to report

Ollie and I were able to locate the warehouse the alien artifact from that article was taken to

but it was gone

yeah sorry

but it did track back to LuthorCorp

yup

that means Lex probably has it

definitely

and he's probably found a way to apply its technology to the trophies

whatever it is

we just arrived in Smallville so we'll check back in later

SEND

Ken'ts
THANKS FOR THE MILK AND COOKIES!
ANYTHING FOR CLARK'S FRIENDS.
NOM
NOM
ABOUT THAT . . . CLARK IS MISSING.
NOM
IT WOULDN'T BE THE FIRST TIME. HE HAS A HABIT OF GOING TO FAR-OFF PLACES AND FINDING HIS WAY BACK.
ALSO, HIS SECRET, AND ALL OF YOURS, IS SAFE WITH US.
WHY DON'T I SHOW YOU ALL SOMETHING DOWN IN THE SHED. FOLLOW ME . . .

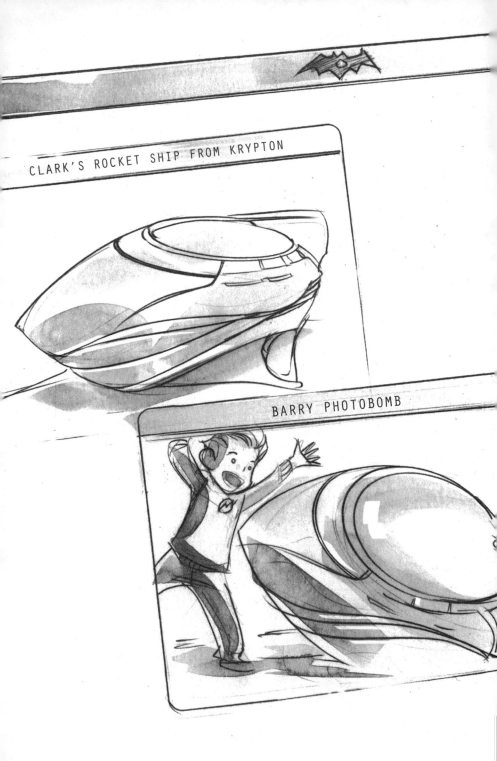

CLARK'S ROCKET SHIP FROM KRYPTON

BARRY PHOTOBOMB

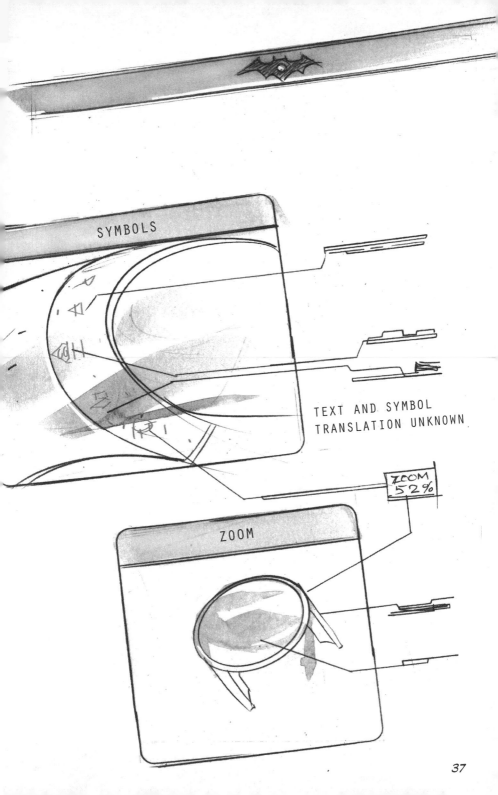

SYMBOLS

TEXT AND SYMBOL
TRANSLATION UNKNOWN

ZOOM
52%

ZOOM

GROUP CHAT

Clark's trophy wasn't the only trophy given out at the ceremony

oh man you're right!

if the others get activated

they might disappear too

can you warn Alfred?

hold on

Alfred? are you there?

Where have you been? I've been worried sick!

not now

look I need you to not touch the trophies

They're not going to clean themselves, Master Bruce.

JUST DON'T TOUCH THE TROPHIES!!!

< USER HAS LOGGED OFF >

SEND

WE NEED TO GET BACK TO THE MANSION BEFORE ALFRED DOES SOMETHING DANGEROUS . . . LIKE DUSTING.
YEAH, I HATE DUST.
BUT IT'LL TAKE TOO LONG TO WAIT FOR THE BUS.
BARRY CAN CARRY US!
I CAN?
HE CAN GET US BACK FASTER BY RUNNING. OLLIE AND VIC CAN MEET US THERE.
WHOOOOOSH
WE SHOULD'VE DONE THIS *BEFORE* I ATE THAT TRIPLE CHEESEBURGER AND DRANK ALL THOSE MALTS! GUH!!
WHERE ARE THEY?
YOU KNOW MY BEDROOM IS STRICTLY OFF-LIMITS!
I PUT THE TROPHIES IN YOUR ROOM.
IN YOUR *OTHER* ROOM.

WHOOOA!
WHY DO YOU HAVE A DINOSAUR TOY HERE?
I'M STILL IN THE PROCESS OF COLLECTING THINGS FOR THE CAVE, OKAY?
HERE'S SOMETHING TO ADD TO YOUR COLLECTION.
A PENNY? UM . . . THANKS?

CLARK WAS RIGHT. YOU DID HAVE A BATCAVE UNDER YOUR HOUSE.
WELL, CLARK'S A SNOOP! BUT I STILL WANT HIM TO COME BACK.
WAIT . . . THE TROPHIES!
GOOD, THEY'RE HERE.
I'LL HAVE THE COMPUTER TAKE A CLOSER LOOK AT THEM.

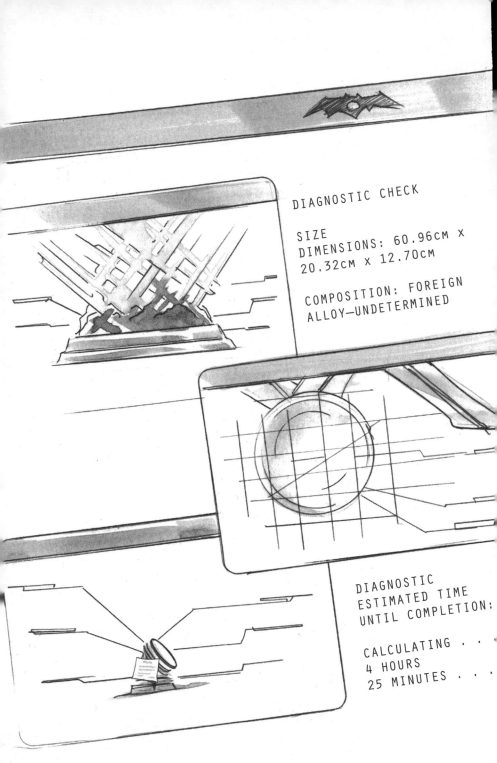

DIAGNOSTIC CHECK

SIZE
DIMENSIONS: 60.96CM X
20.32CM X 12.70CM

COMPOSITION: FOREIGN
ALLOY—UNDETERMINED

DIAGNOSTIC
ESTIMATED TIME
UNTIL COMPLETION:

CALCULATING . . .
4 HOURS
25 MINUTES . . .

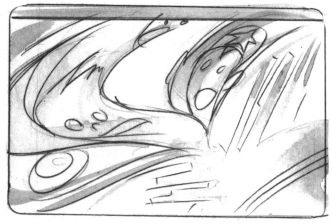

WELCOME TO DETENTION.
THERE IS NO WAY OUT.
SUFFER.
WELCOME TO DETENTION.
THERE IS NO WAY OUT.
SUFFER.
WELCOME TO DETENTION.
THERE IS NO WAY OUT.
SUFFER.

WHAT HAPPENED?!
YOUR TEMPER GOT US SENT HERE!
SORRY. WHERE'S "HERE"?
WHEN I HACKED INTO THE LUTHORCORP COMPANY RECORDS, THERE WAS A FILE LISTED AS "LEX PHANTOM DETENTION."
IF THIS IS LEX'S IDEA OF DETENTION, WE HAVE VERY DIFFERENT IDEAS. THIS IS UNLIKE ANY I'VE BEEN IN . . . AND I'VE BEEN TO A LOT!
I KNOW ALL ABOUT THAT.
WELCOME TO DETENTION. THERE IS NO WAY OUT. SUFFER.

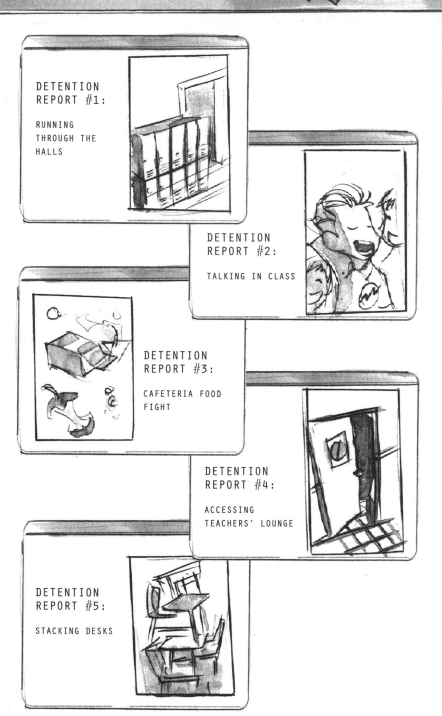

DETENTION
REPORT #1:

RUNNING
THROUGH THE
HALLS

DETENTION
REPORT #2:

TALKING IN CLASS

DETENTION
REPORT #3:

CAFETERIA FOOD
FIGHT

DETENTION
REPORT #4:

ACCESSING
TEACHERS' LOUNGE

DETENTION
REPORT #5:

STACKING DESKS

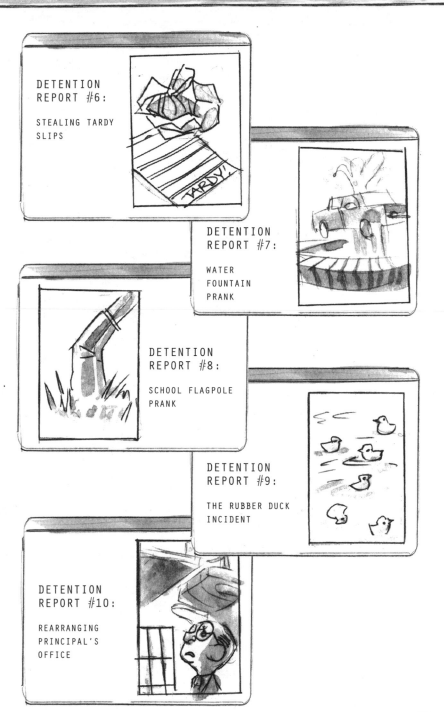

DETENTION
REPORT #6:

STEALING TARDY
SLIPS

DETENTION
REPORT #7:

WATER
FOUNTAIN
PRANK

DETENTION
REPORT #8:

SCHOOL FLAGPOLE
PRANK

DETENTION
REPORT #9:

THE RUBBER DUCK
INCIDENT

DETENTION
REPORT #10:

REARRANGING
PRINCIPAL'S
OFFICE

49

THIS DESERT IS ENORMOUS. WHAT DIRECTION SHOULD WE GO IN?
I'LL MAKE A PATH. JUST FOLLOW ME!
WHAT'S WRONG?
I CAN'T RUN. I DON'T HAVE ANY SUPER-SPEED!
NNNGH! I DON'T HAVE ANY STRENGTH, EITHER!
CLANGG
THWOF

THERE'S SOMETHING ABOUT THIS DETENTION THAT IS NULLIFYING YOUR POWERS.
IT'S A GOOD THING I'VE NEVER NEEDED ANY.
JERK!
AWWW, WE'RE ALL DOOMED!
UM, EVERYONE . . . WHAT'S THAT?

ROBOTIC DRONE!

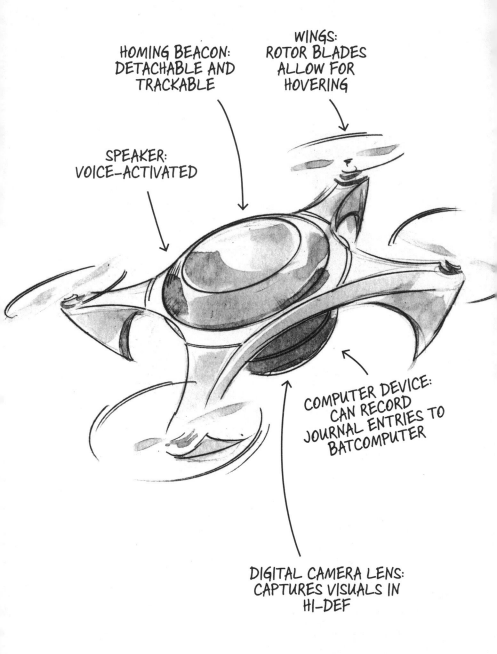

HOMING BEACON:
DETACHABLE AND
TRACKABLE

WINGS:
ROTOR BLADES
ALLOW FOR
HOVERING

SPEAKER:
VOICE-ACTIVATED

COMPUTER DEVICE:
CAN RECORD
JOURNAL ENTRIES TO
BATCOMPUTER

DIGITAL CAMERA LENS:
CAPTURES VISUALS IN
HI-DEF

USERNAME: BWAYNE
RE: JOURNAL ENTRY 2

WE'VE FOUND OURSELVES TRANSPORTED INTO THIS PHANTOM DETENTION. IT'S PRESUMABLY THE SAME PLACE CLARK DISAPPEARED INTO, ALTHOUGH WE HAVEN'T SEEN HIM.

THIS PLACE IS PRETTY BARREN. IT'S LIKE A BEACH WITHOUT THE FUN, OR SO I'M TOLD BY BARRY AND HIS NEED FOR HUMOR TO LIGHTEN THE MOOD.

LUCKILY MY ROBOTIC DRONE AND BATCOMPUTER WERE SUCKED INSIDE WITH THE REST OF US. THEY'RE ALLOWING ME TO RECORD THESE JOURNALS AS WELL AS PROVIDE OTHER HELPFUL TOOLS AS WE NAVIGATE HERE.

ANOTHER THING ODD ABOUT THIS PLACE IS NO ONE CAN USE THEIR POWERS. BARRY CAN'T MOVE SUPER-FAST, EVEN IF HE'S ANNOYING AT ANY SPEED. DIANA'S STRENGTH IS GONE. VIC'S CYBERNETIC PARTS ARE UNRELIABLE AND FALLING APART. AND OLIVER'S TARGETING SKILLS ARE OFF, ALTHOUGH IT MIGHT BE DUE TO THE GRAVIMETRIC PROPERTIES OF THIS DIMENSION.

STILL . . . I HOPE WE CAN FIND CLARK AND GET OUT OF HERE. I MISS MY CAVE.

WHAT IS IT?
A DRONE I'VE BEEN WORKING ON AT HOME.
DOES IT HAVE A NAME?
I'M THINKING SOMETHING WITH "BAT" IN THE TITLE.
YOU SHOULD TRY SOMETHING DIFFERENT.
NAME IT AFTER A BIRD, LIKE A MAJESTIC EAGLE.
NAHHH. IT'S SMALL, SO YOU SHOULD NAME IT AFTER A SMALL BIRD. LIKE A RED ROB—
NO. I DON'T WANT A BIRD FOR A SIDEKICK.

WHOA, IS THAT A HOMING BEACON?
WE'LL NEED IT IF WE WANT TO FIND OUR WAY BACK.
WHERE ARE WE GOING?
IT'S CLARK. HE'S GOT TO BE HERE.
AND WE'VE GOT TO FIND HIM AND BRING HIM BACK.

My name is Clark Kent and I'm lost. I have no idea where I am or how I got here. But I've been trying to find a way out. I've walked in many directions, but this place is playing tricks with my eyes. I think I'm just walking in a circle.

I hope someone reads this who can help me out. Maybe even my friends. Thanks!

USERNAME: BWAYNE
RE: JOURNAL ENTRY 3

CLARK IS HERE! WE HAVEN'T SEEN HIM YET BUT WE FOUND A
NOTE THAT HE LEFT BEHIND FOR US. IT MAKES ME WONDER HOW
MANY OTHER PEOPLE MIGHT BE STUCK HERE, TOO.

IT'S IMPOSSIBLE TO TRACK ANYONE IN THIS SAND. OR
IT COULD BE THAT WE HAVEN'T BEEN ABLE TO FIND ANY
FOOTPRINTS. BUT IF CLARK KEEPS LEAVING NOTES, THEN MAYBE
THEY'LL LEAD US RIGHT TO HIM.

I HOPE WE CAN FIND HIM QUICKLY. THERE'S A REASON WHY
PEOPLE STAY OUT OF THE DESERT. IT'S UNBEARABLY HOT,
UNCOMFORTABLE, AND WALKING ACROSS THE SHIFTING SAND CAN
MAKE ONE FEEL NAUSEOUS. THIS DETENTION HAS THE EFFECT
THAT I MISS SCHOOL, OR AT LEAST ALFRED. IF HE WERE HERE,
HE'D BE ABLE TO BRING ME SOMETHING COLD TO DRINK.

ME AM HERE
WHERE AM HERE
HERE AM WHERE
YOU AM PLEEZ LOOZ ME

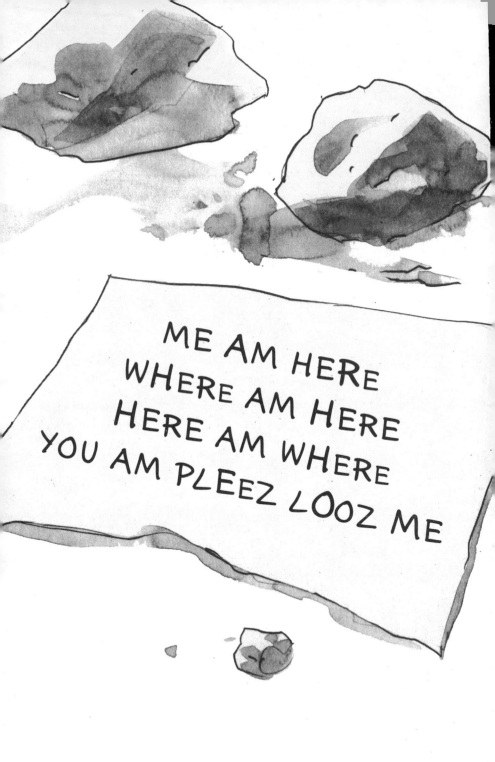

This is Clark again. I think. I'm not the only one stuck here. I think others are trapped here as well. Sometimes I notice shapes moving in the distance that look like people. There's also weird messages scribbled on rocks.

I'm going to try to find anyone else who's here. Maybe together we can find a way out.

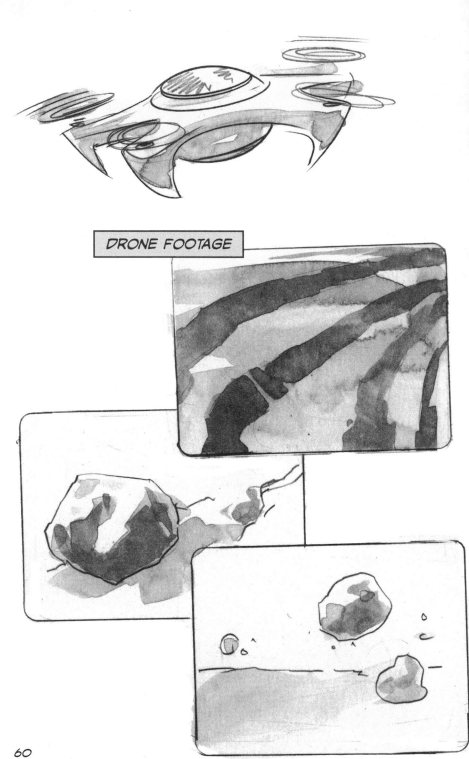

DRONE FOOTAGE

COVER YOUR EYES AND TRY TO KEEP UP!
ALL THIS SAND . . . IS GETTING IN MY GEARS.
I'VE GOT IT MUCH WORSE. IT'S IN MY SHOES. BLEHH!
GOOD-BYE
CLARK? IT'S CLARK!!

ME NO AM CLARK
ME AM BIZARRO

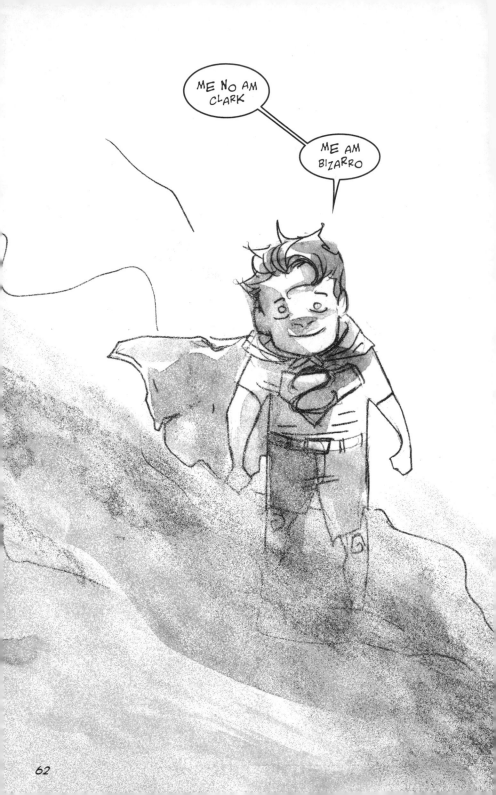

USERNAME: BWAYNE
RE: JOURNAL ENTRY 4

WE FOUND CLARK . . . KIND OF. OKAY, NOT REALLY.

THIS KID LOOKS A LITTLE LIKE CLARK . . . IF HE HAD FALLEN OFF HIS TRACTOR BACK ON THE FARM. AND THEN THE TRACTOR DROVE OVER HIM. MULTIPLE TIMES. OVER AND OVER.

HIS NAME IS BIZARRO AND HE SPEAKS FUNNY. ALMOST SAYING WORDS THAT HAVE THE OPPOSITE MEANING. MAKING IT TOUGH TO UNDERSTAND WHAT HE'S SAYING AT TIMES. IT MAKES ME WONDER HOW HE GOT HERE.

HE SEEMS HARMLESS ENOUGH. AND HE'S JOINED US, FOLLOWING ALONG LIKE A PUPPY DOG, AS WE CONTINUE TO LOOK FOR CLARK.

Comparison Chart

Clark
Bizarro
Shy
Not Shy
S
Backward S
Speaks in full Sentences
Speaks backward

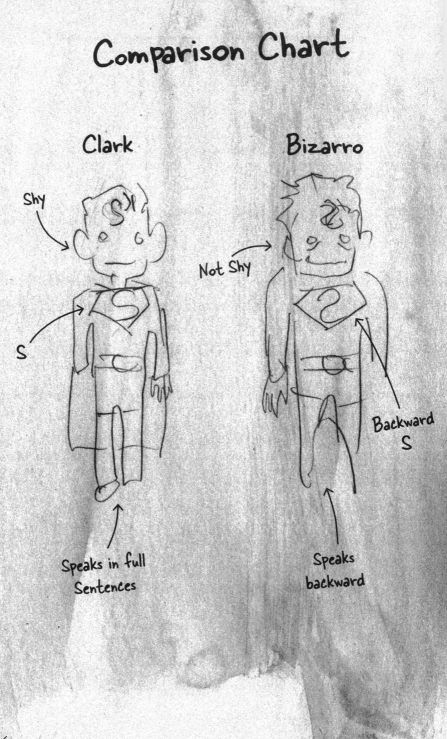

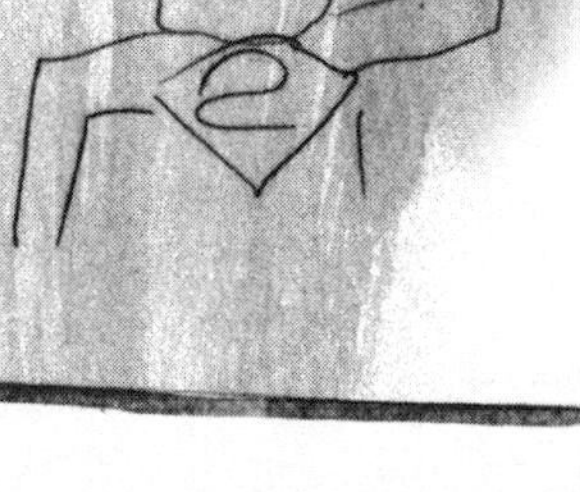

ME AM LEARN YOU HOW SPEAK AM ME AM USE FIVE HARD STEPS

1) ME AM ME ← (me = you)

(you = me)

2) YOU AM YOU

3) THEY AM THEY ← (they = they)

NOW YOU AM BIZARRO LIKE ME AM ←
           (Now you are Bizarro like I am)

BOOoo AND CLAP LEGS
           (Cheer and clap hands)

YOU AM FAIL BECOME BIZARRO

(You have become Bizarro)

WHO ARE YOU?
YOU AM NOT BIZARRO
ME AM BIZARRO
LET'S TRY THIS AGAIN. HOW DID YOU—
AHEM!
HOW AM ME GET HERE?
ME AM NOT KNOW
FANTASTIC.
HEY, WE FOUND ANOTHER!

I still can't find a way out or anyone else. And my head feels a little woozy. I can't tell up from down in this place.

I don't even have ~~powers~~ I mean, I don't have the power to do anything in here. I hope my friends find me. But if they do, they'll probably be stuck, too. So maybe it's for the best if they don't find me.

This is my last note. If you find this, go back. You'll better off than me.

DETENTION DANGERS

NO DIVING
OFF CLIFFS!

WATCH YOUR
STEP!
CANYONS!

NO GOLFING
HERE—
SANDPITS!

BEWARE
YOUR
SHADOW . . .
ANY SHADOWS

YEAH, THAT STUFF'S BAD.
BUT HEY . . .
NO HOMEWORK.
AM I RIGHT?!
ALARM SCREEN . . .
LIGHTS . . .
CAUTION . . .
MOTION DETECTOR . . .
SOMETHING APPROACHING

SHADOWS ARE EVERYWHERE EVERYWHERE
EVERYWHERE
THEY FOLLOW FOLLOW FOLLOW
DON'T LET THEM TOUCH YOU
STAY OUT OF THE DARK DARK DARK

THE GROUND IS MOVING!
NO, THEY'RE SHADOWS!
LEAVE HIM ALONE!
THANKS, DIANA. I JUST WASN'T FAST ENOUGH.
THWUPP
THEY AM GOOD
THEY AM VERY GOOD

CRONKK
BACK UP!
WE'RE OUT OF ROOM!
WHUMP
LEAVE MY FRIENDS ALONE!
CLARK!

THESE PHANTOMS CAN'T BE HURT. BUT THEY CAN BE SCARED AWAY.
I'VE SO GOT THIS!
NOT THAT WAY. THEY'RE ONLY AFRAID OF THE LIGHT.
HEY!
SPARK
FWOOOSH
I REALLY SHOULD MAKE THAT FIRE RESISTANT.

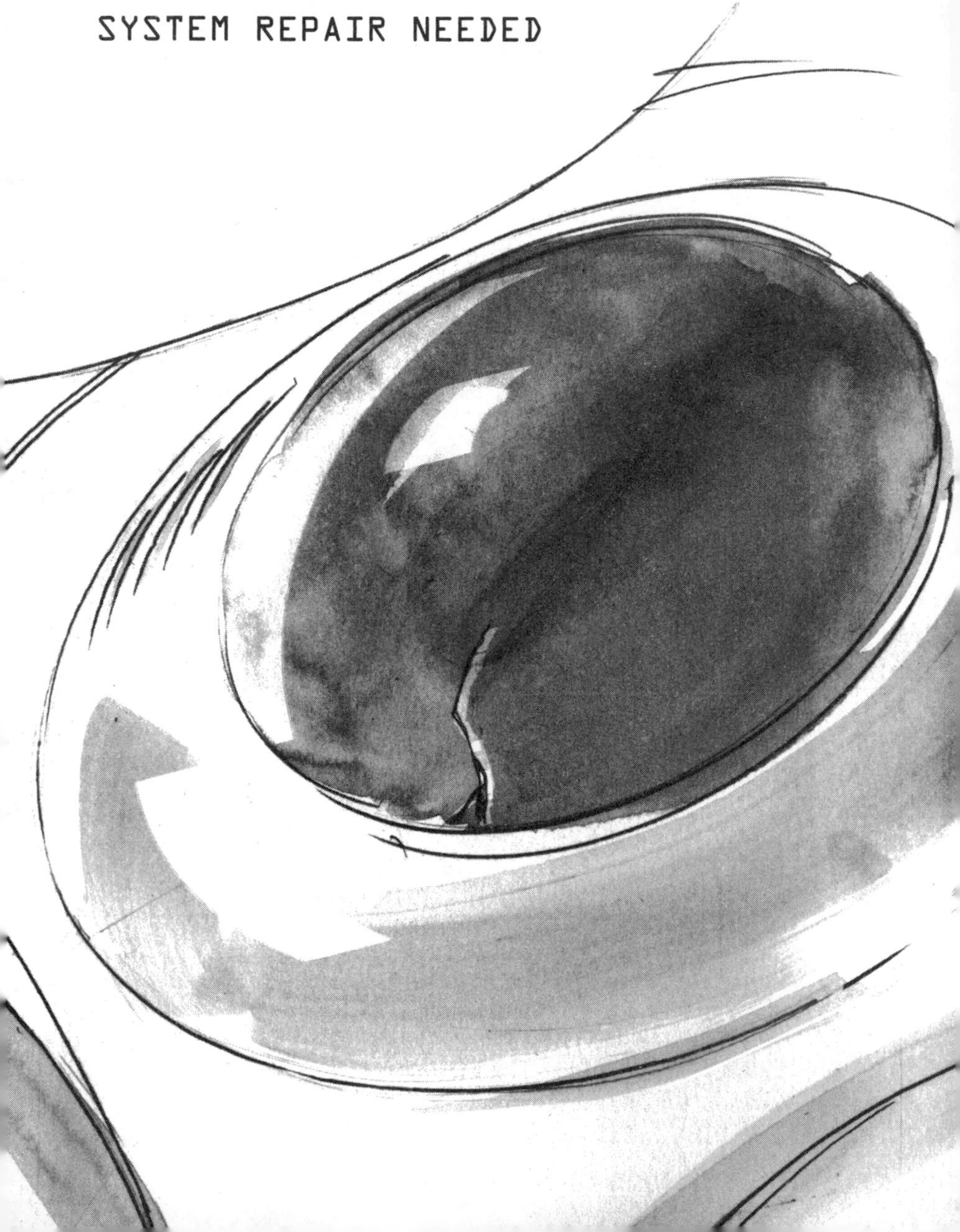

HOMING BEACON INACCESSIBLE
DAMAGE TO TARGETING UNIT
FUNCTIONALITY 0%
SYSTEM REPAIR NEEDED

THEY WEAR CLOAKS THAT HIDE THEIR FACES.
WHATEVER HAPPENS, DON'T LET THEM TOUCH YOU!
THEY'RE AFRAID OF LIGHT AND FIRE BUT NOTHING ELSE.
PAY ATTENTION TO YOUR SURROUNDINGS! STAY AWAY FROM THE DARK AND DON'T GET CAUGHT STANDING IN ANY SHADOWS OR THEY'LL GRAB YOU!

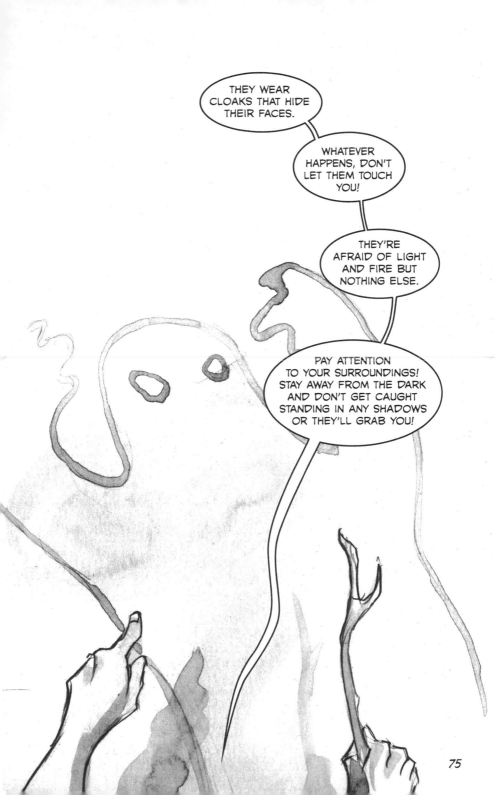

USERNAME: BWAYNE
RE: JOURNAL ENTRY 5

WE WERE ABLE TO FIND CLARK! DIANA TELLS ME IT WAS CLARK
WHO FOUND US. I DON'T CARE. I'M JUST HAPPY HE'S OKAY.

THIS DETENTION REALLY HAS PHANTOMS AFTER ALL! THEY COME
OUT OF THE SHADOWS AND ARE LIKE GHOSTS. WE'RE UNABLE TO
FIGHT THEM, BECAUSE IF WE GET TOUCHED, THEY CAN STEAL
OUR SPIRIT . . . AT LEAST THAT'S WHAT CLARK BELIEVES.
THE ONLY THING THAT SCARED THEM AWAY WAS CREATING A
TORCH FOR LIGHT. I JUST WISH CLARK HADN'T DESTROYED MY
BAT COSTUME IN THE PROCESS. IT'S THE ONLY ONE I BROUGHT
WITH ME.

AND MORE BAD NEWS IS, THE DRONE WAS DAMAGED DURING THE
FIGHT. ITS HOMING BEACON DOESN'T WORK. IF WE CAN'T
REPAIR IT, WE WON'T BE ABLE TO FIND OUR WAY BACK.

CLARK SAYS THERE ARE OTHERS HERE WHO ARE STUCK IN
DETENTION. HE WANTS US TO RESCUE THEM, TOO. IT LOOKS
LIKE WE'VE GOT OUR WORK CUT OUT FOR US!

BARRY'S DETENTION GUIDE:
GETTING TO KNOW YOUR DETENTIONS

DETENTION

report to homeroom
for detention

sit at desk and wait
for bell to leave

get yelled at by
teachers

no passing notes

sit at desk with nothing
to do

find friends in
detention

avoid spitballs

PHANTOM DETENTION

get sucked inside scary
dimention

sit in sand and never leave

get chased by Phantoms

no use of powers

walk in desert and be lost

find friends in phantom
detention

avoid sandstorms

THIS SANDSTORM MAKES IT HARD TO SEE WHERE WE'RE WALKING!
IF I HAD MY BATSUIT, THIS WOULDN'T BE A PROBLEM!
I SAID I WAS SORRY ABOUT THAT!
ARGUE LATER! FIND SHELTER NOW!
A CAVE IS A GOOD PLACE TO TAKE COVER.
HOW'S ABOUT IN THERE? LET'S GO!

THE WRITING ON THIS SIGN IS KRYPTONIAN.
WHAT DOES IT SAY?
I'M NOT SURE.
MAYBE THIS WILL OPEN IT.
BZZRRT
WELCOME, KAL-EL.

KAL-EL?
I GUESS THAT MEANS "OPEN SESAME" IN KRYPTONIAN.

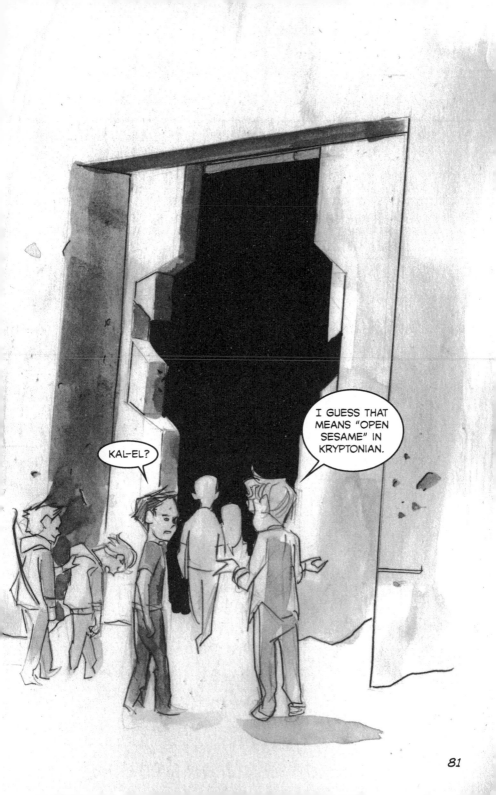

KRYPTON PREP ACADEMY WAS THE BEST SCHOOL IN THE GALAXY FOR HIGHER EDUCATION.
BUT EVEN IN THIS UTOPIA FOR LEARNING, THERE WERE SOME STUDENTS WHO THREATENED TO RUIN THE PROGRAM.

SO THE PHANTOM DETENTION WAS CREATED, AS A ZONE TO HOLD BAD STUDENTS SO THEY MIGHT REFLECT ON THEIR ACTIONS.

THE HOUSE OF EL WAS RESPONSIBLE FOR BUILDING THE PHANTOM PROJECTOR TO SEND BAD STUDENTS THERE.

BEWARE THE PHANTOM DETENTION! IT CAN PLAY TRICKS ON YOUR MIND OR CREATE BACKWARD DUPLICATES TO FOOL YOU. THOSE UNWILLING TO LEARN FROM THEIR MISTAKES ARE DOOMED TO BECOME PHANTOMS.

USERNAME: BWAYNE
RE: JOURNAL ENTRY 6

THE KRYPTONIAN MUSEUM WE FOUND FOR SHELTER FROM THE
SANDSTORMS EXPLAINED A LOT. WE'RE STUCK HERE IN THIS
PHANTOM DETENTION.

LUTHORCORP MUST'VE RECOVERED THE PROJECTOR TECHNOLOGY
AS PART OF THE SPACE DEBRIS THEY COLLECTED IN
SMALLVILLE FOLLOWING THE METEOR SHOWER. AND ONCE LEX
FOUND OUT WHAT HIS FATHER HAD, HE FOUND A WAY TO
INSTALL THIS PHANTOM DETENTION PROJECTOR INTO CLARK'S
TROPHY TO SEND HIM AND THE REST OF US HERE.

I'M GOING TO GET OUT OF HERE, AND WHEN I DO, I'M
GOING TO TAKE LEX LUTHOR DOWN! AND I'LL HAVE HELP. WE
DISCOVERED SOME ITEMS IN THE SAND THAT LED US TO OTHER
KIDS TRAPPED HERE. I JUST NEVER THOUGHT IT WOULD BE
THEM . . .

ITEMS FOUND IN SAND

TEETH

JOKER FISH

CLOWN YOYO

FLOWER PRANK

LOOK AT ALL THIS STUFF.
AND IT LEADS THAT WAY.
HAAAAAALP! WE'RE STUCK IN THIS SANDPIT!
STAY STILL SO I CAN USE YOUR HEAD TO STEP OUT OF HERE!
EEEP!
COME ON, LET'S GO.
WE CAN'T JUST LEAVE THEM.
WHY NOT?
THEY'RE JUST AS STUCK HERE AS WE ARE. IF WE CAN HELP THEM, THEN WE SHOULD.
AND THEY MIGHT BE ABLE TO HELP US FIND A WAY OUT.
ANY ESCAPE OUT OF DETENTION IS ALWAYS WELCOME!
FINE, FINE . . . BUT I DON'T HAVE TO LIKE IT.

MAYBE IF WE JOIN HANDS.
THEN WE ALL MIGHT FALL IN. WE NEED SOMETHING STRONGER TO HOLD US.
DON'T WORRY. I'LL JUST FLY IN AND GET THEM.
CLARK, YOU DON'T HAVE POWERS IN THE PHANTOM ZONE!
NOPE NOPE NOPE . . . IT'S CALLED THE PHANTOM DETENTION.
WAAAAHHHHH

HOLD ON!
WE'VE GOT YOU, TOO!
THIS WOULD BE FUNNY IF IT WEREN'T SCARY. HEE HEE HEE.

USERNAME: BWAYNE
RE: JOURNAL ENTRY 7

IT APPEARS CLARK WAS RIGHT. WE'RE NOT THE ONLY ONES STUCK HERE. BUT THE JOKER AND HARLEY AREN'T WELCOME COMPANY. HOW CAN I FORGET ALL THE TIMES THEY PULLED PRANKS ON ME AT SCHOOL? PULLING OUT MY CHAIR. THROWING PIES AT ME. THE FOOD FIGHTS IN THE CAFETERIA.

EVERY TIME THEY'RE AROUND, THEY'RE NOTHING BUT TROUBLE. BUT CLARK FEELS SORRY FOR THEM AND WANTS TO GIVE THEM A CHANCE. PLUS, WE CAN USE ALL THE HELP WE CAN GET TRYING TO FIND A WAY OUT.

SINCE I CONSIDER THEM MORE LIKE SUSPECTS THAN FRIENDS, MAYBE IT'S TIME TO PUT MY DETECTIVE SKILLS TO USE. TRY TO FIND OUT WHAT THEY KNOW AND IF IT'S ANY HELP TO US . . .

GCPD JUNIOR DETECTIV
INTERROGATION NOTES

SUBJECTS: THE JOKER AND HARLEY
CRIME: WRONG PLACE, WRONG TIME
SUSPECTS: UNDETERMINED

THE JOKER AND HARLEY WERE FOUND INSIDE THE
PHANTOM DETENTION, CLAIMING TO BE PRISONERS.
THEIR EXCUSE WAS THAT LEX WANTED TO RECRUIT
THEM INTO HIS LITTLE BAD GUY GANG, BUT THEY
DIDN'T WANT TO HAVE ANYTHING TO DO WITH IT.
THE JOKER FOUND THE WHOLE THING TO BE A LAUGH
RIOT. HARLEY FELT ALLERGIC TO CATS, EVEN
THOUGH CHEETAH JUST WEARS A CATSUIT.

LEX DIDN'T CARE FOR THEIR REASONS AND
TOOK OFFENSE. SO HE OPENED UP THE PHANTOM
DETENTION AND KEPT THEM PRISONER HERE. ONCE
HE KNEW IT WORKED, HE USED THE TECHNOLOGY TO
PLAN HIS CAPTURE OF CLARK AND THE REST OF US.

THEY ALSO DON'T KNOW HOW TO GET OUT OF THE
PHANTOM DETENTION.

HARD TO KNOW IF THEY'RE TELLING THE TRUTH.
THEY'VE ALWAYS BEEN OBNOXIOUS AND CLASS
CLOWNS. BUT I'LL GO ALONG WITH IT FOR NOW.

YOU CAN COME ALONG. BUT ONLY IF YOU DON'T CAUSE ANY TROUBLE.
WE PROMISE!
HERE'S PHANTOM ZONE IN YOUR EYE, KID.
HEY! OW.
IS IT TOO LATE TO THROW THEM BACK IN THE SANDPIT?

USERNAME: BWAYNE
RE: JOURNAL ENTRY 8

ONE OF THE THINGS I'VE NOTICED IS THAT TIME HAS NO MEANING IN PHANTOM DETENTION. THE SUN DOESN'T SET. IT FEELS LIKE WE'VE BEEN WALKING FOR DAYS OR WEEKS. MAYBE EVEN LONGER. OR IT COULD BE ONLY MINUTES THAT ARE STRETCHED OUT. IT'S HARD TO KNOW FOR SURE, SINCE THERE ARE BROKEN CLOCKS EVERYWHERE.

FOR NOW, THE JOKER AND HARLEY ARE PART OF OUR GROUP. I THINK THEY'RE MORE TROUBLE THAN THEY'RE WORTH, ALWAYS JOKING AND PRANKING AND LAUGHING. BUT I REALIZE THEY'RE STUCK IN HERE JUST LIKE WE ARE. AND IF WE CAN ALL FIND THE EXIT AND GET OUT TOGETHER, THEN THAT'S A WORTHY GOAL.

JUST NO MORE PIES OR SAND IN MY FACE!

WHY THE LONG FACE, HARL, WHEN YOU CAN CAST A LONG SHADOW INSTEAD?
HAH HEH HEHHH!
WAS IT SOMETHING I SAID?!
PHANTOMS!!
FOR MY NEXT JOKE, I'LL NEED A CHIMPANZEE, A SKATEBOARD, AND A WATER PISTOL.
MISTA J! YOU'RE SINKING!

GAAAAHHHHHH!
BARRY!
GET HIM!
I LOST MY PUDDIN'.
AND WE LOST BARRY.

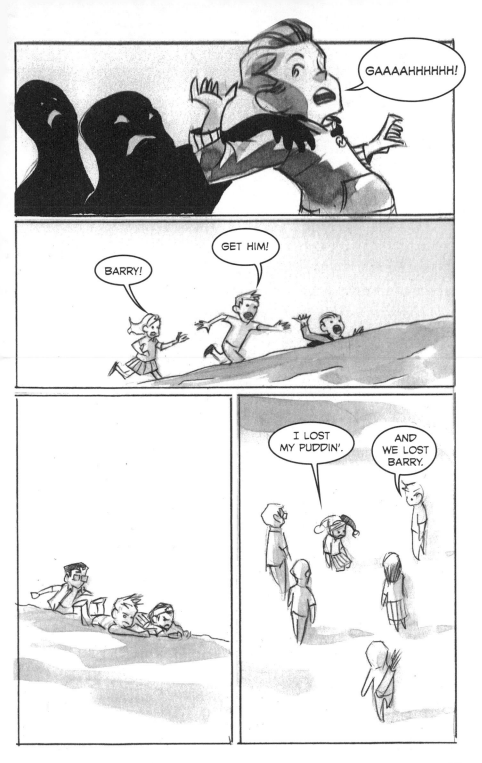

USERNAME: BWAYNE
RE: JOURNAL ENTRY 9

THIS PHANTOM DETENTION IS REALLY DANGEROUS! EVERY
SHADOW HAS THE POSSIBILITY OF A PHANTOM HIDING IN
IT. WHEN WE WEREN'T PAYING ATTENTION, THE PHANTOMS
APPEARED AND KIDNAPPED BARRY AND THE JOKER. WITH-
OUT THOSE TWO AROUND TO CONSTANTLY TALK, JOKE, AND
ANNOY, IT'S A LOT MORE QUIET. IN A WAY, I KIND OF
LIKE IT. BUT IT'S NO REASON FOR THEM TO BE TAKEN.

WE NEED TO FIND BOTH OF THEM AND GET THEM BACK AND
THEN FIND A WAY OUT OF HERE. WE'VE BEEN HERE LONG
ENOUGH. AND THE LONGER WE'RE STUCK HERE, THE WORSE
IT GETS.

PLUS, I'VE GOT A CAVE I STILL NEED TO FIX UP.

KRYPTONIAN MUSEUM

CLIFF

MOUNTAINS

SANDPIT

PHANTOM
SIGHTING

THE JOKER

BARRY

BIZARRO HAS BEEN IN THIS PHANTOM DETENTION THE LONGEST. HE MIGHT HAVE AN IDEA WHERE OUR FRIENDS WERE TAKEN.
WHO WANTS TO ASK HIM?
NOT ME. I CAN'T EVEN UNDERSTAND HIM.
DON'T LOOK AT ME. I FIRE ARROWS, NOT QUESTIONS.
I TALK TO COMPUTERS. I'M NOT SO GREAT WITH PEOPLE.

UH, HARLEY . . . ?
BIZARRO SAYS WE SHOULD GO TO THE SHADOWLANDS. HE AM RIGHT!
WAIT! HOW DID YOU FIND OUT?
I JUST ASKED HIM, SILLY. HE'S NOT THAT HARD TO UNDERSTAND.
BUT WHERE ***ARE*** THE SHADOWLANDS?!
BIZZY WILL DRAW YA A MAP. PROBLEM SOLVED.

ME AM TOUR GUIDE TO SHADOWLANDS
AVOID ON PATH
FRIENDS AM HERE
NO TOUCH GHOST OR BE GHOST
IF AM GHOST, THEN RETURN TO BODY TO ARRIVE FROM SHADOWLANDS

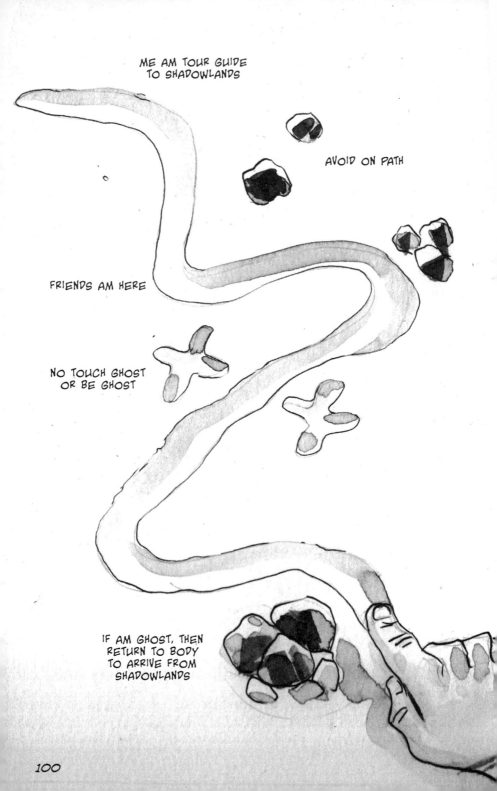

YOU AM HERE.
SO, ACCORDING TO HIS MAP, THERE ARE GHOSTS HERE THAT TURN US INTO GHOSTS IF THEY TOUCH US? GREAT.
WHOA, THIS MUST BE THE "TIME-OUT" ROOM. GET IT? BECAUSE THE CLOCK IS BROKEN.
I HATE DETENTION!
MAYBE IT'S BEST FOR US TO STAY CLOSE SO WE DON'T GET SEPARATED IN THE DARKNESS.

GOOD IDEA. LET'S HOLD HANDS.
UM . . . THAT'S NOT WHAT I MEANT.
WE CAN USE THAT TO TIE EVERYONE TOGETHER.

SCAN AREA INDETERMINATE
TARGET LOCATIONS UNKNOWN

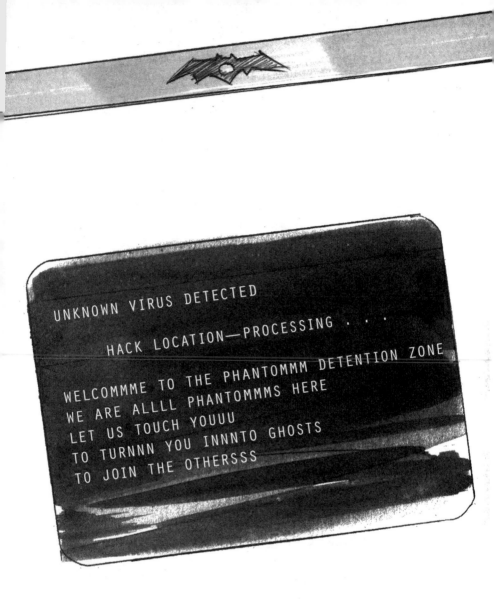

UNKNOWN VIRUS DETECTED

HACK LOCATION—PROCESSING . . .

WELCOMMME TO THE PHANTOMMM DETENTION ZONE

WE ARE ALLLL PHANTOMMMS HERE
LET US TOUCH YOUUU
TO TURNNN YOU INNNTO GHOSTS
TO JOIN THE OTHERSSS

USERNAME: BWAYNE
RE: JOURNAL ENTRY 10

I'M WRITING THIS IN DARKNESS WITH ONLY THE DRONE SCREEN
LIGHT TO HELP ME SEE. THIS LIGHT MIGHT COME IN HANDY
FOR MORE THAN JUST WRITING, SO I'M GOING TO WRITE DOWN
AS MUCH AS I CAN TO KEEP IT ON.

WE ENTERED THE SHADOWLANDS IN SEARCH OF OUR MISSING
FRIENDS AND TOOK PRECAUTIONS TO STAY TOGETHER. BUT ONE
AFTER THE OTHER STARTED TO DISAPPEAR. AND NOW I'M THE
LAST ONE AND ALL ALONE.

BY MYSELF, IN THE DARK . . . YOU WOULD THINK I'D LIKE
THIS. NORMALLY I'D AGREE, BUT NOT THIS TIME. I NEED MY
FRIENDS. AND I WILL FIND THEM ALL, EVEN IF I HAVE TO DO
IT BY MYSELF.

WHEN THESE PHANTOMS TOUCH ANYONE, THEY TAKE THEIR
BODIES TO "TIME-OUT" WHILE THEIR GHOSTS WANDER AND
REMAIN LOST. BUT I'M ALWAYS PREPARED FOR ANYTHING.
I THINK I CAN USE MY COMPUTER TO HELP FIND EVERYONE
AND GET THEM BACK TO NORMAL SO WE CAN GET OUT OF THIS
DETENTION. AT LEAST I THINK I CAN. I'VE NEVER ACTUALLY
DONE THIS BEFORE, SO WISH ME LUCK!

ALFRED WOULD LAUGH EVERY TIME I LOCKED MYSELF IN THE
CLOSET OR HID UNDER THE BED. OR THOSE TIMES I WOULD GO
DOWN INTO THE BATCAVE AT NIGHT WITHOUT A FLASHLIGHT.
I'D USE THE EXCUSE THAT I WAS SLEEPWALKING, WHEN REALLY
I WAS JUST TRAINING MYSELF TO SEE BETTER IN THE DARK.
NOW ALL THAT TRAINING IS ABOUT TO PAY OFF.

THESE PHANTOMS LIKE THE DARKNESS, BUT SO DO I. AND
THERE'S NO WAY I'M GETTING STUCK IN DETENTION WITHOUT
RESCUING MY FRIENDS.

THESE PHANTOMS PICKED THE WRONG KID TO PICK ON!
I'M GOING TO RUN A SONAR GHOST LOCATING PROGRAM ON MY
DRONE. THEY WON'T SEE THIS COMING . . .

GHOST LOCATOR MODE — ACTIVATED
< RUN ECHOLOCATION PROGRAM >

(GHOST LOCATION: 100%)

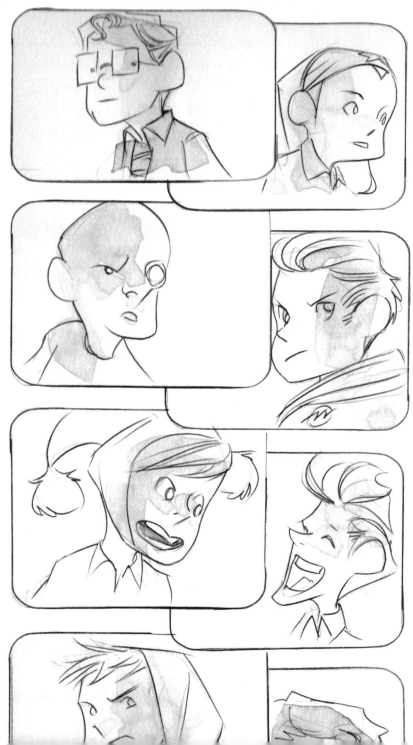

GHOSTS SITTING AT DESKS? THAT'S A NEW ONE.
DIANA, WAKE UP!
CLARK? ANYONE?
I KNEW YOU WERE HERE. BUT I'M TOO FAST FOR YOU.
TOO AGILE FOR YOU.

AND . . .
TOO SMART
FOR YOU.
SKREEEEEE

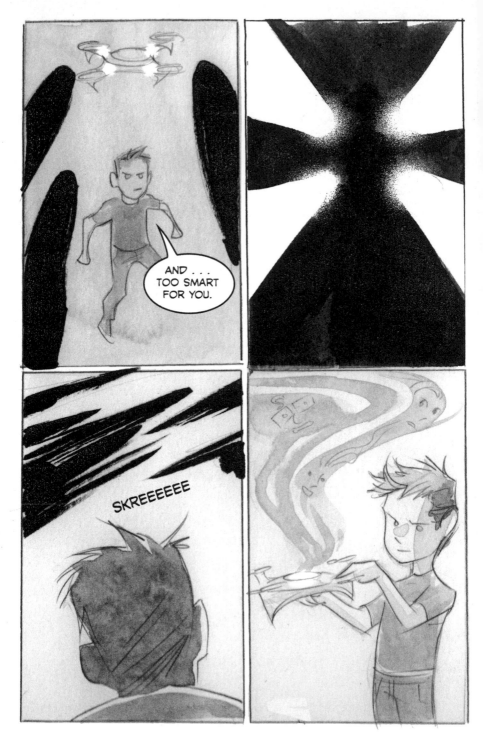

YAWN
YAWN
YAWN
WHOA . . . I HAD THIS NIGHTMARE THAT I WAS IN DETENTION, AND THEN—
WAIT . . . I'M STILL IN DETENTION!
RELAX, BARRY. YOU'RE FREE NOW.

USERNAME: BWAYNE
RE: JOURNAL ENTRY 11

I'VE SEEN A LOT OF CRAZY THINGS. VILLAINS. EVIL ROBOTS. ALIENS. MONSTERS. BUT I NEVER THOUGHT I'D SEE GHOSTS. ALFRED WOULD SAY I LIVE A CHARMED LIFE. AND I WOULD TELL ALFRED . . . YES, NOW CAN WE PLEASE ORDER PIZZA?

I WAS LUCKY TO BE ABLE TO FIND ALL MY FRIENDS. ONCE I DEFEATED THE PHANTOMS, EVERYONE TURNED BACK TO THEIR NORMAL SELVES. IT WAS WEIRD.

NOW THAT WE'RE OUT OF THE SHADOWLANDS, IT'S TIME TO FIX MY DRONE. WITHOUT A WORKING HOMING BEACON, WE'D BE STUCK HERE FOREVER. AND IT'S PAST TIME WE GOT OUT OF HERE!

Cooling fan needs to be cleaned of dirt. Give this to Barry. He'll be the hamster to spin this wheel. —Bruce
I CAN REPLACE THIS CRACKED MONITOR SCREEN USING SOME OF MY OWN PARTS. —VIC
Ollie's arrowheads can help tighten any screws down. —Bruce
I CAN FIX THE HOMING BEACON CIRCUITRY SO IT'S NOT EXPOSED. —VIC
All these tangled wires need to be untangled. This one's for Diana. —Bruce

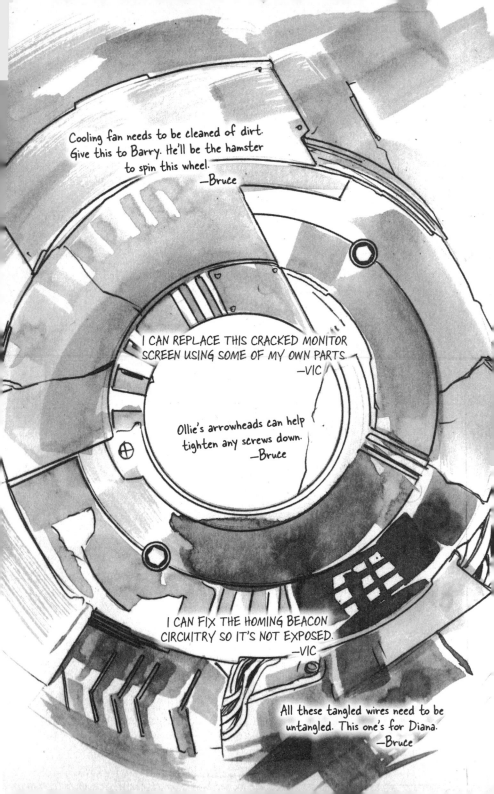

SYSTEM DIAGNOSTIC COMPLETE
DRONE OPERATING AT FULL CAPACITY
HOMING BEACON LOCATED

GOOD JOB, EVERYONE! WE FIXED IT TOGETHER.
AND NOW I'LL REAP THE REWARDS. OR RIP THEM FROM YOU.
ME TOO, MISTA J.
HEE HEE HEEEEE
MY DRONE AND MY COMPUTER, TOO?! ARGHH!!

OKAY, YOU WERE RIGHT. THOSE TWO ARE NOTHING BUT TROUBLE.
FORGET IT. ALL I CARE ABOUT IS GETTING MY STUFF BACK.
IF WE DON'T, WE HAVE NOTHING TO HELP US FIND OUR WAY OUT.
HOW DO WE DO THAT? THEY CAN BE ANYWHERE OUT IN THIS DESERT.
JUST LIKE BEFORE, WE FOLLOW THEIR TRACKS. AND HOPE FOR NO MORE SANDSTORMS.

TRACKING SUSPECTS

EVERYONE LEAVES TRACKS WHEREVER THEY GO. THESE ARE SOME HELPFUL THINGS TO KEEP IN MIND WHILE TRACKING YOUR SUSPECT:

- KNOW THE TRACKS OF THE PERSON YOU'RE TRYING TO FIND
- ELIMINATE OTHER TRACKS TO NARROW YOUR SEARCH
- DON'T EXPECT TO FIND PERFECT TRACKS
- LOOK FOR HEEL MARKS
- THE TOE WILL NOT LEAVE A HEAVY PRINT
- PEOPLE PUT THEIR FEET UP WHEN THEY RELAX, SO LOOK AROUND
- MARKS CAN BE LEFT WHEN CLIMBING OVER OBSTRUCTIONS
- PEOPLE DIG IN THEIR TOES MORE WHEN WALKING ON AN INCLINE
- PATTERNS CAN TRANSFER FROM ONE SURFACE TO ANOTHER

- THE SPACES BETWEEN FOOTPRINTS ARE LONGER FOR RUNNING, SHORTER FOR WALKING
- DON'T GET FOOLED IF TRACKS CROSS ONE ANOTHER
- LOOK AROUND FOR ANYTHING INTERRUPTED
- CLUES ARE EVERYWHERE

Why stand around listening to your voice drone on when I can just take your drone with me
Thanks, Brucie!
—J
I love this computer! Can I play games on it, too?
-Harl

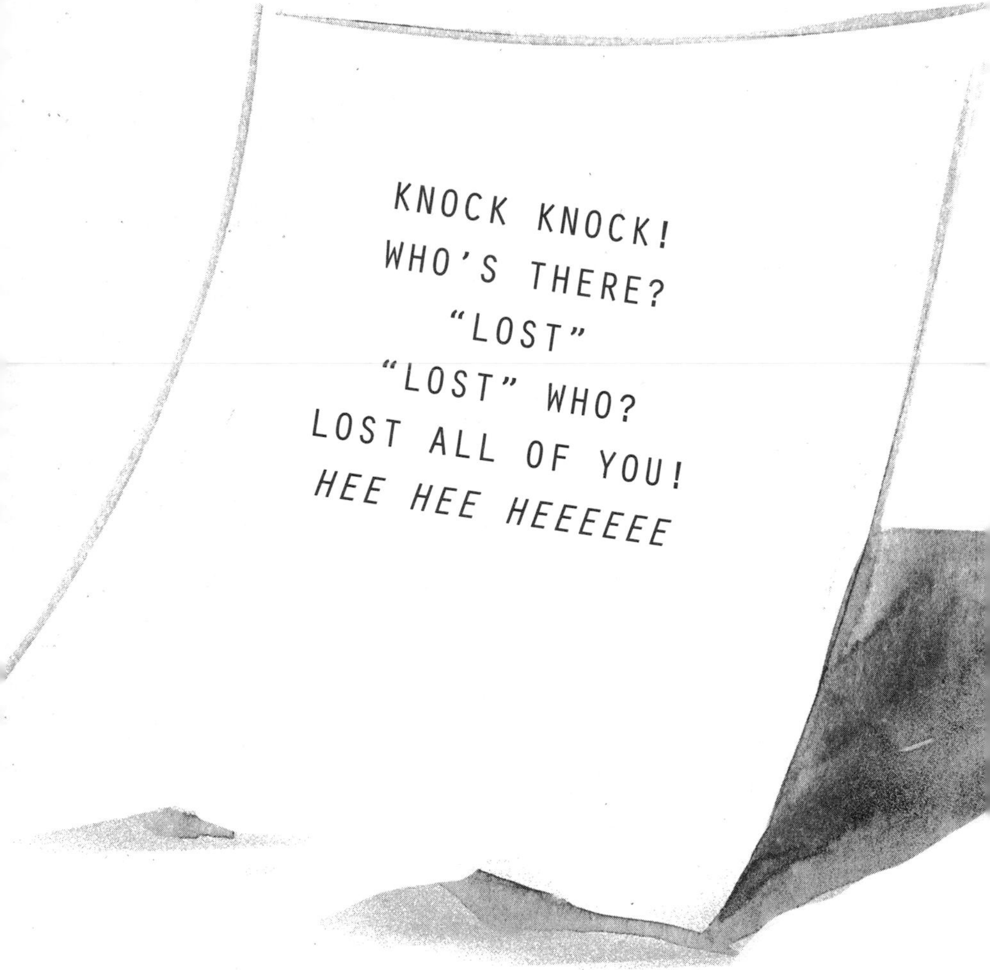
KNOCK KNOCK!
WHO'S THERE?
"LOST"
"LOST" WHO?
LOST ALL OF YOU!
HEE HEE HEEEEEE

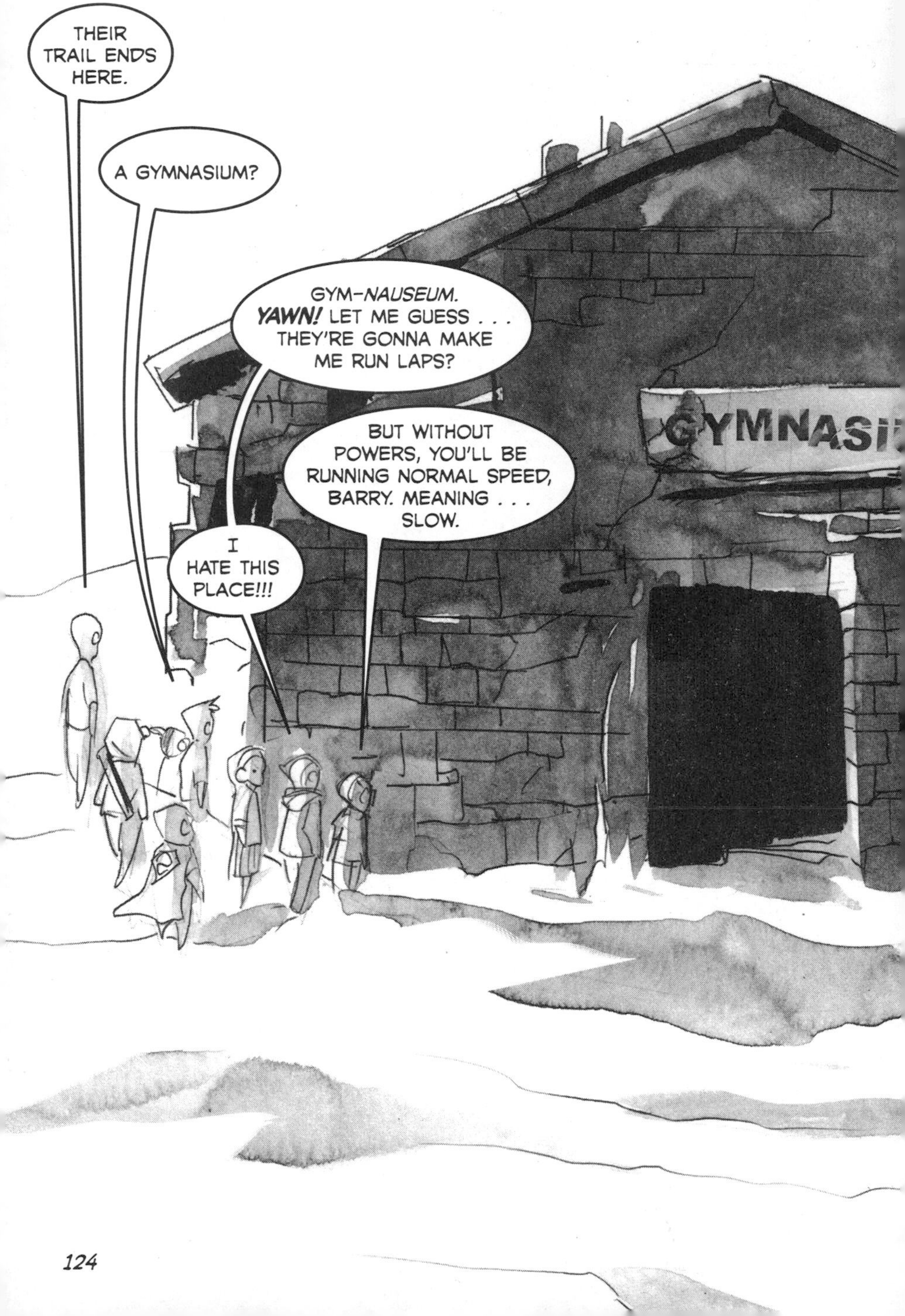
THEIR TRAIL ENDS HERE.
A GYMNASIUM?
GYM-*NAUSEUM.* ***YAWN!*** LET ME GUESS . . . THEY'RE GONNA MAKE ME RUN LAPS?
BUT WITHOUT POWERS, YOU'LL BE RUNNING NORMAL SPEED, BARRY. MEANING . . . SLOW.
I HATE THIS PLACE!!!
GYMNASI

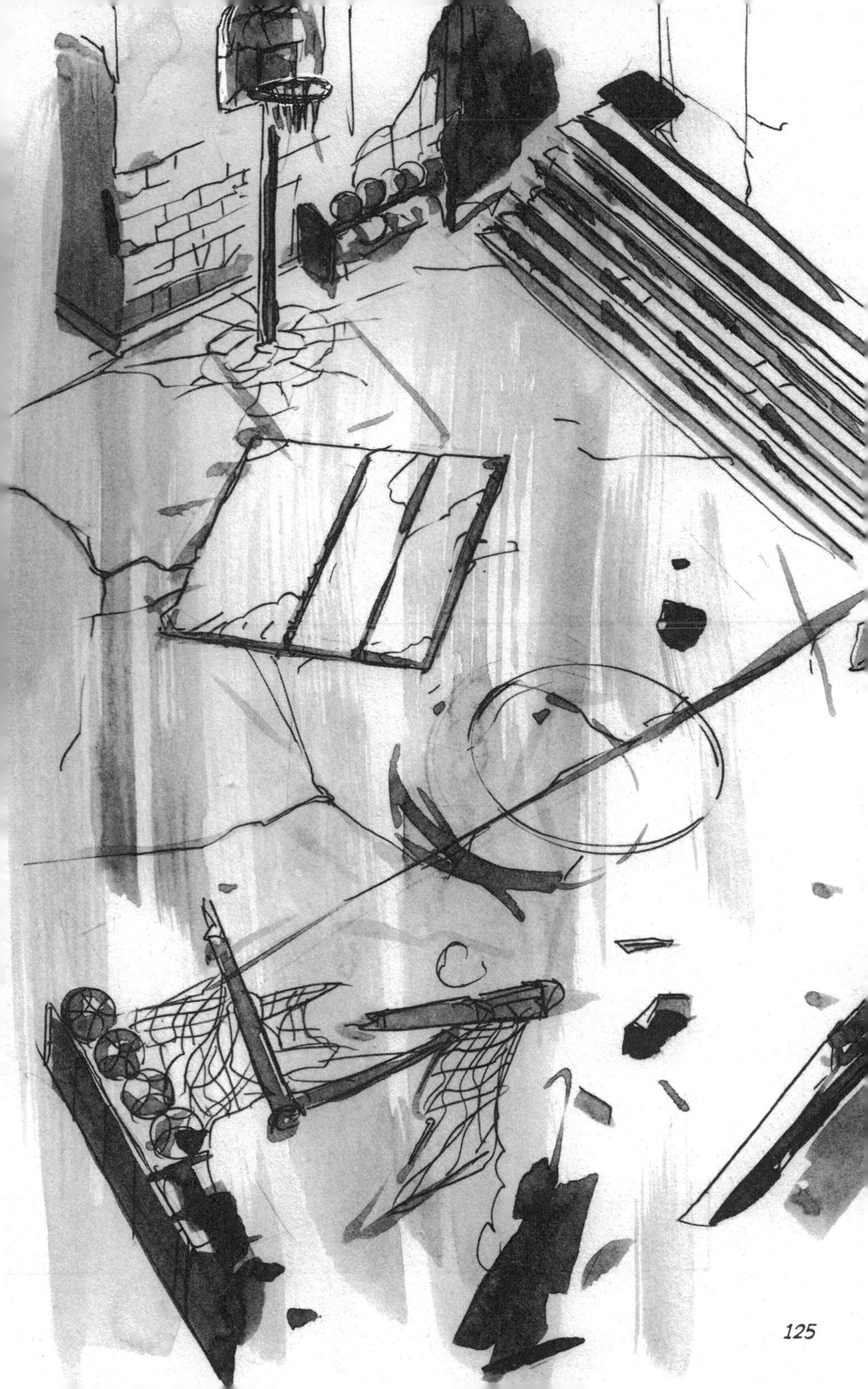

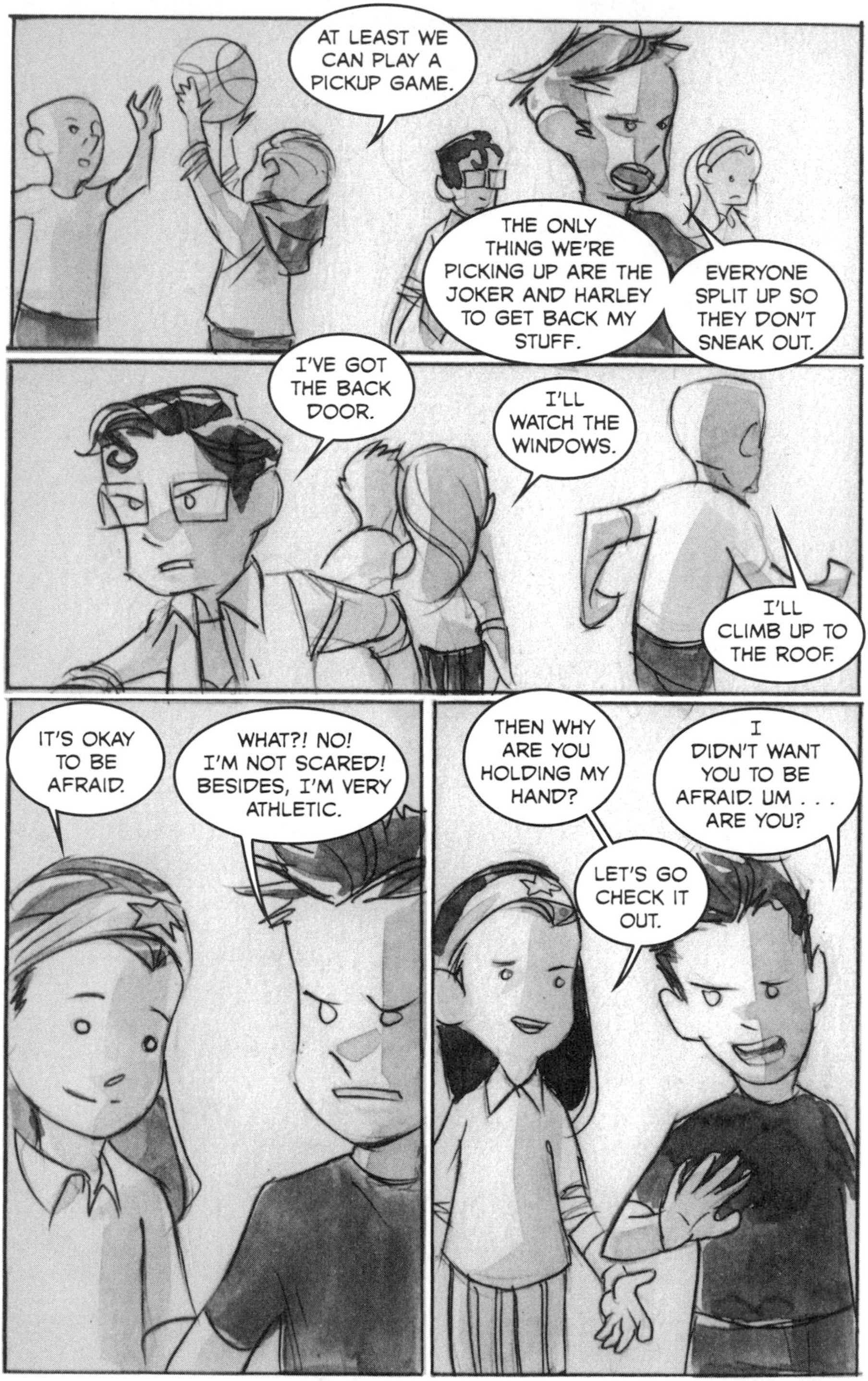
AT LEAST WE CAN PLAY A PICKUP GAME.
THE ONLY THING WE'RE PICKING UP ARE THE JOKER AND HARLEY TO GET BACK MY STUFF.
EVERYONE SPLIT UP SO THEY DON'T SNEAK OUT.
I'VE GOT THE BACK DOOR.
I'LL WATCH THE WINDOWS.
I'LL CLIMB UP TO THE ROOF.
IT'S OKAY TO BE AFRAID.
WHAT?! NO! I'M NOT SCARED! BESIDES, I'M VERY ATHLETIC.
THEN WHY ARE YOU HOLDING MY HAND?
I DIDN'T WANT YOU TO BE AFRAID. UM . . . ARE YOU?
LET'S GO CHECK IT OUT.

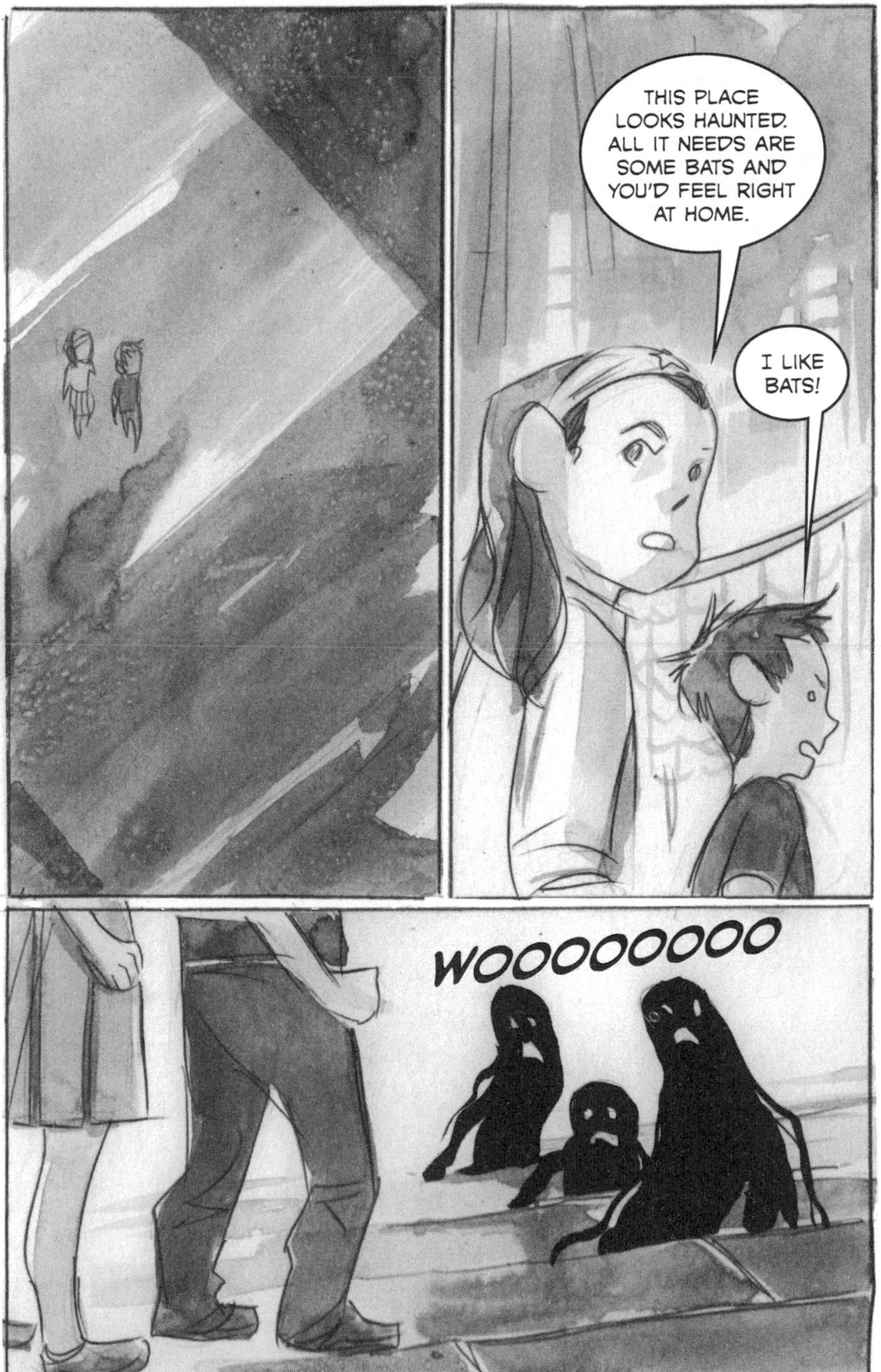
THIS PLACE LOOKS HAUNTED. ALL IT NEEDS ARE SOME BATS AND YOU'D FEEL RIGHT AT HOME.
I LIKE BATS!
WOOOOOOOO

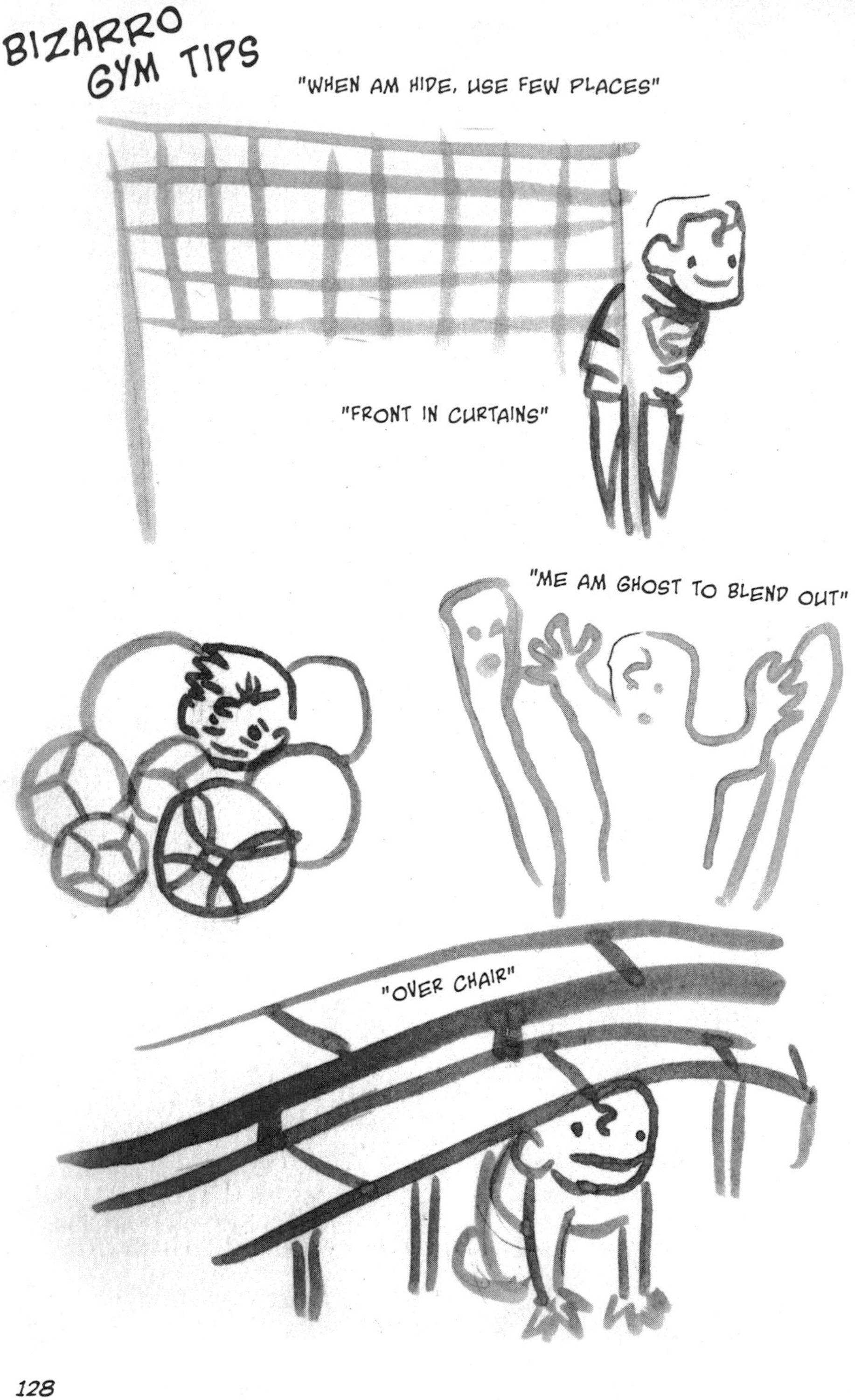
BIZARRO GYM TIPS
"WHEN AM HIDE, USE FEW PLACES"
"FRONT IN CURTAINS"
"ME AM GHOST TO BLEND OUT"
"OVER CHAIR"

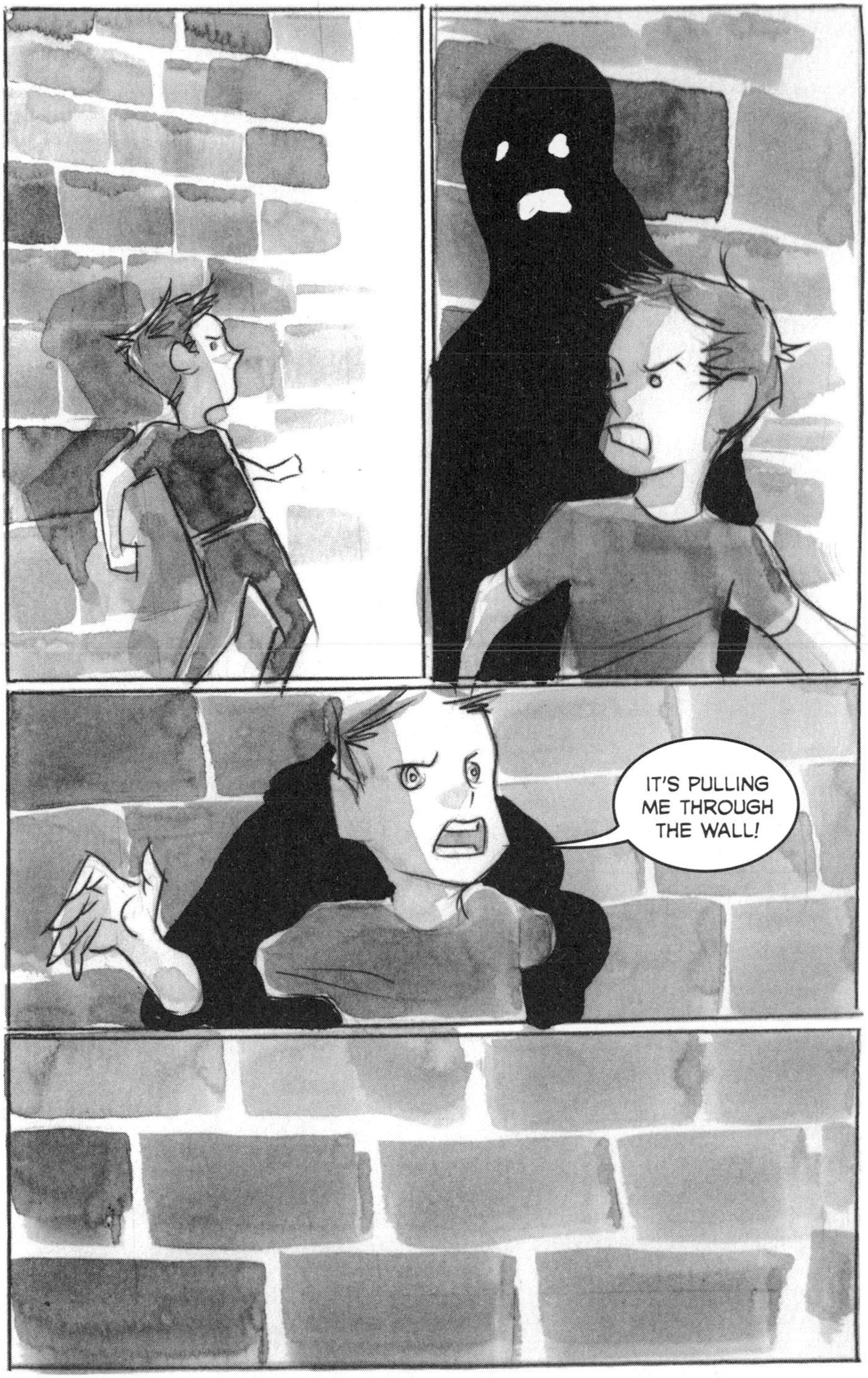
IT'S PULLING ME THROUGH THE WALL!

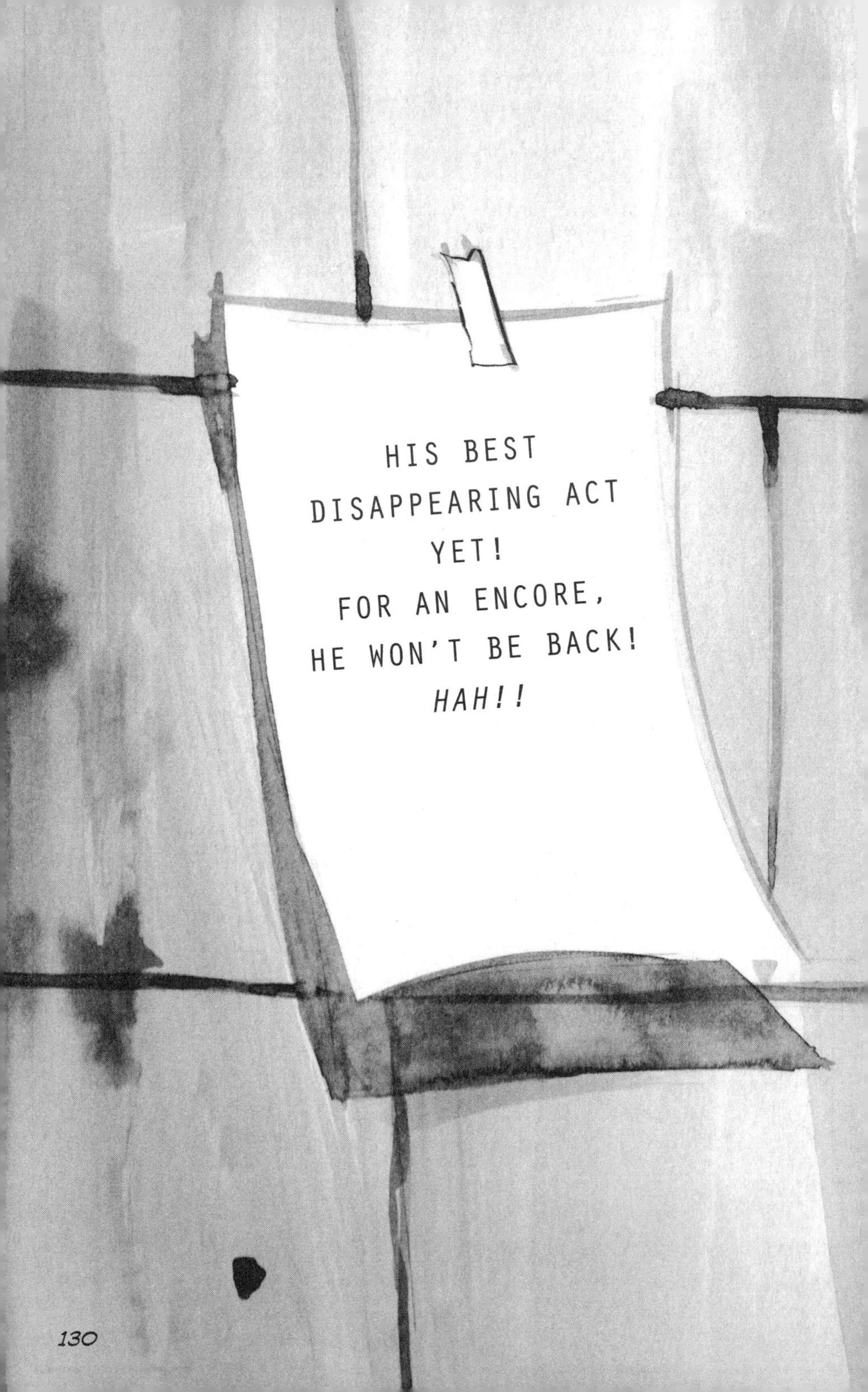
HIS BEST
DISAPPEARING ACT
YET!
FOR AN ENCORE,
HE WON'T BE BACK!
HAH!!

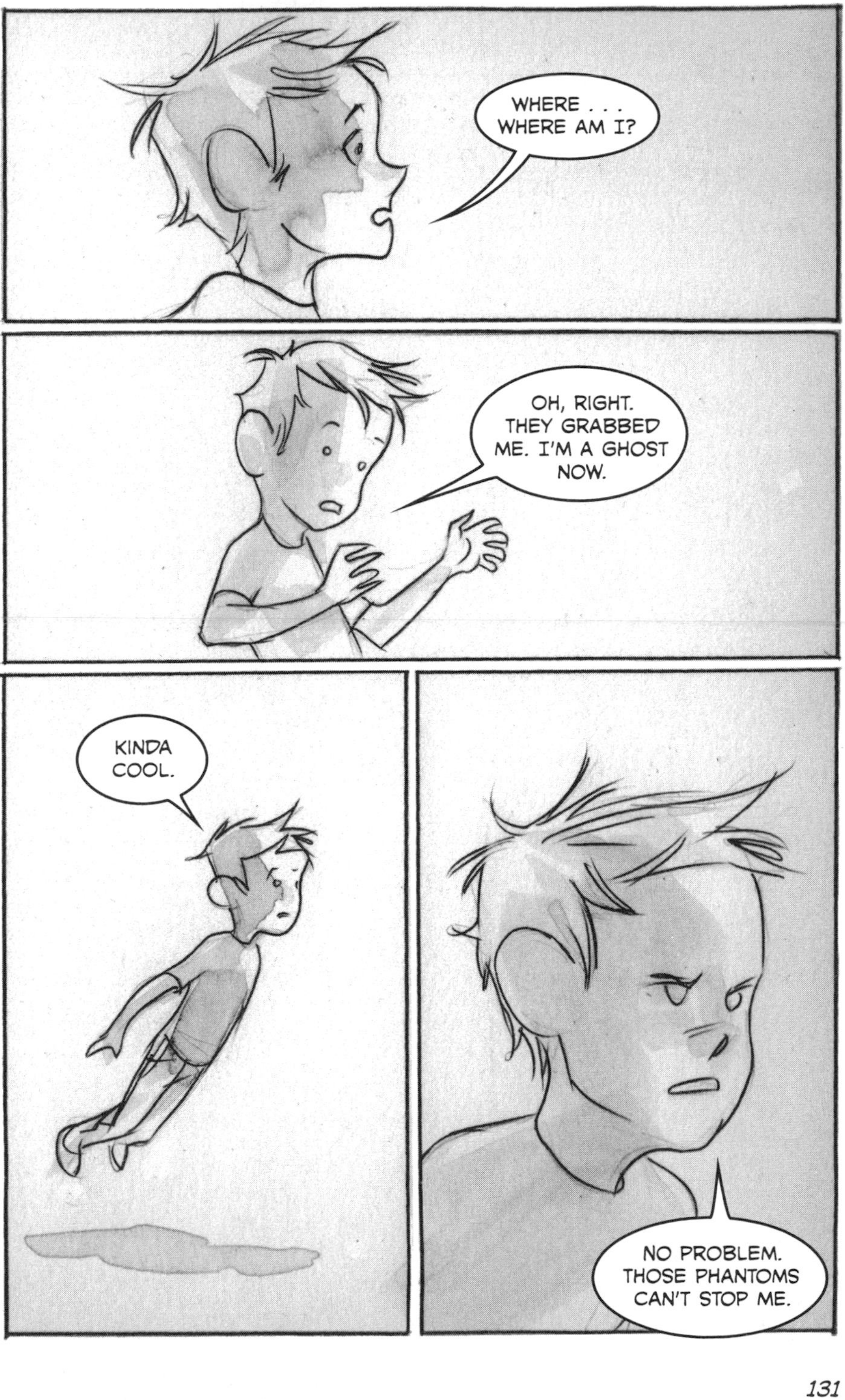
WHERE . . .
WHERE AM I?
OH, RIGHT.
THEY GRABBED
ME. I'M A GHOST
NOW.
KINDA
COOL.
NO PROBLEM.
THOSE PHANTOMS
CAN'T STOP ME.

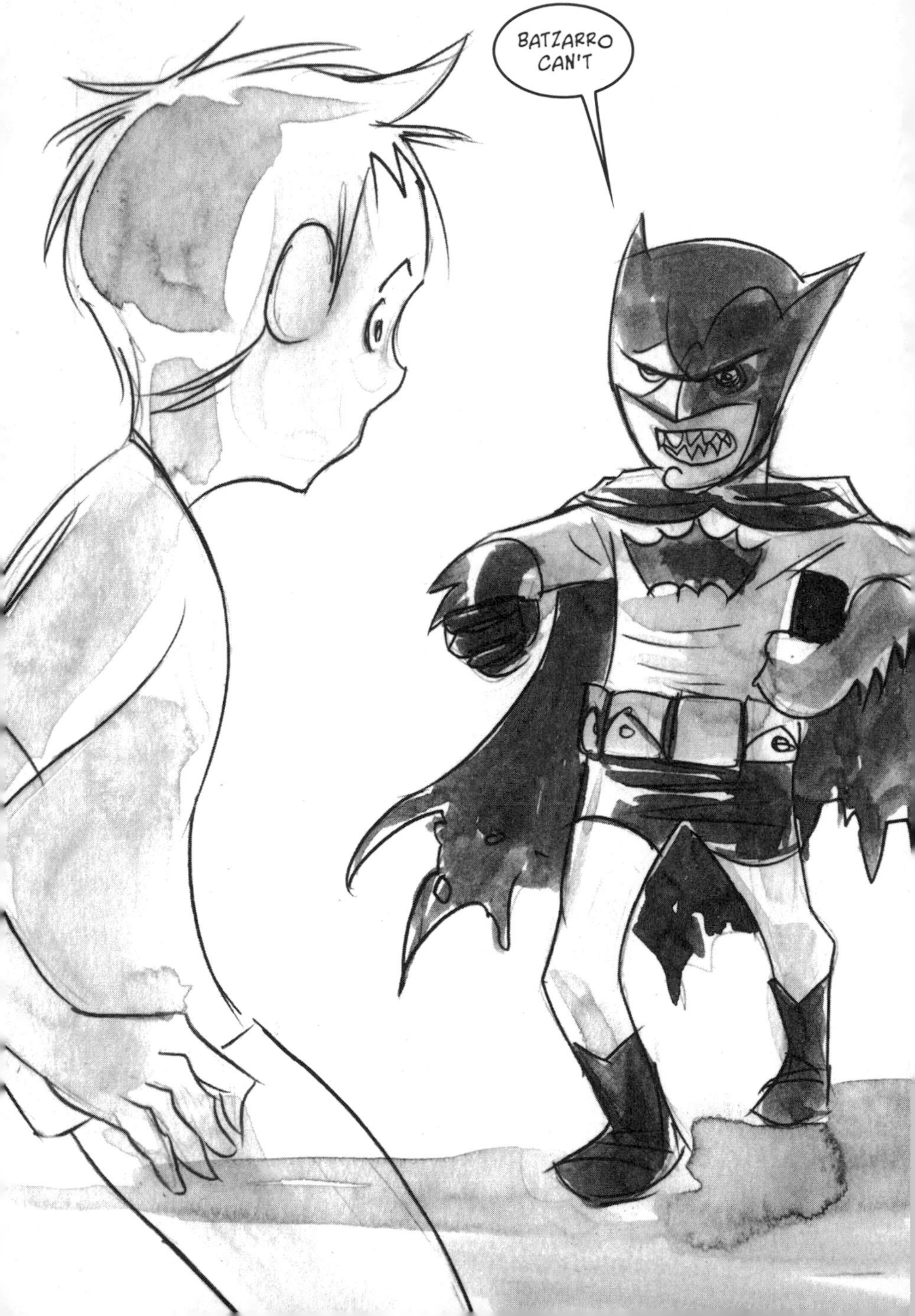
BATZARRO CAN'T

"BATMAN'S GUIDE TO BEATING BATMAN"
BY BATMAN, FOR BATMAN

NO ONE CAN BEAT BATMAN . . . EXCEPT FOR BATMAN.
SO TO BEAT BATMAN, YOU MUST BE BATMAN!
THESE ARE SOME TIPS FOR WHAT TO DO:

1) FIRST YOU MUST BE BATMAN. ALWAYS BE BATMAN.
2) BATMAN KNOWS HOW TO BEAT EVERYONE. KNOW EVERYTHING HE KNOWS.
3) PULL HIS EARS.
4) PULL HIS CAPE.
5) PULL HIS LEG (JOKES HELP, BAD JOKES HELP BETTER).
6) WHEN ALL ELSE FAILS . . . FIGHT DIRTY. BECAUSE HE WON'T.

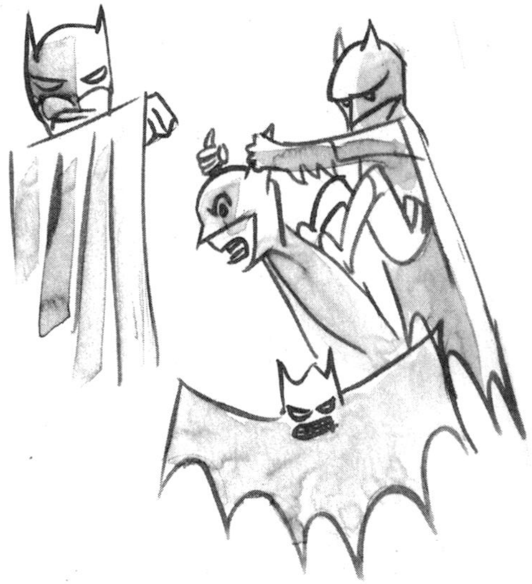

HOW ARE YOU BATMAN?
YOU AM NOT ME
ME AM BATZARRO
YOU AM BATMAN
I TOTALLY AM! AND I ACTUALLY UNDERSTOOD THAT.
THIS PHANTOM DETENTION REALLY CAN PLAY TRICKS ON US.
IT'S CREATED MY OPPOSITE!
ME AM NOT BATMAN!

YOINK
WHAT'S BATMAN'S FAVORITE PART OF THE JOKE?
THE "PUNCH" LINE!
ME NO UNDERSTAND
KRAK

DRONE FOOTAGE: BIZZARO SAVES THE DAY

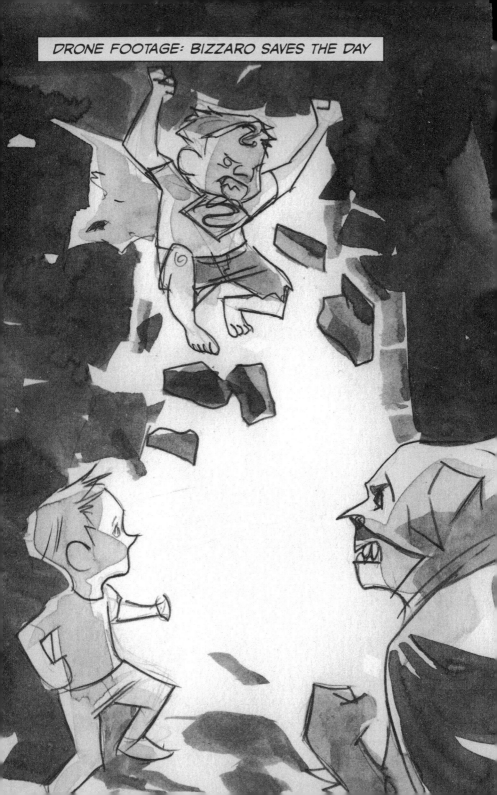

YOU AM BIZARRO ENEMY
YOU AM BATZARRO ENEMY
WORST ENEMIES EVAH
BRUCE! YOU'RE BACK!
THAT WAS WEIRD.

DRONE FOOTAGE: BRUCE HEARS PHANTOMS

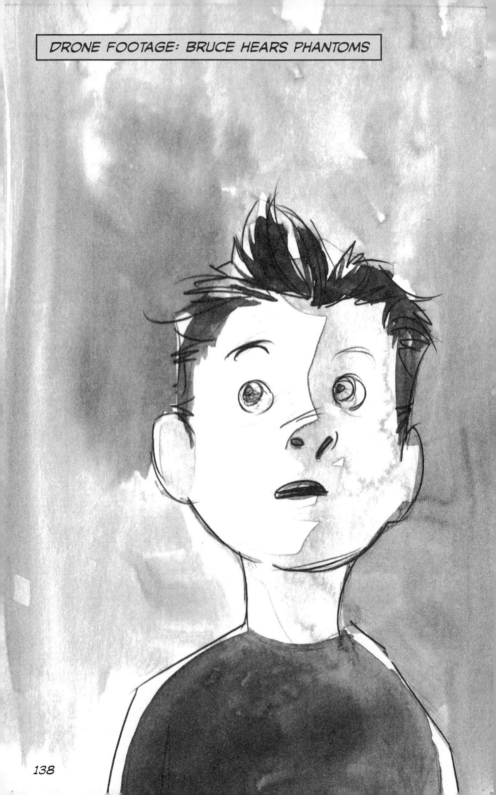

YOU CAN'T ESCAPE DOOMSDAY . . .
COME BAAACK
I GOTTA GET OUT OF HERE, DIANA!
BRUCE, WAIT!
YOU WILL MAKE A GREAT ADDITION TO USSS
YOU CANNOT GET AWAAAAY

MY DRONE?!
SKREEEEEE
DEFINITELY MY DRONE!

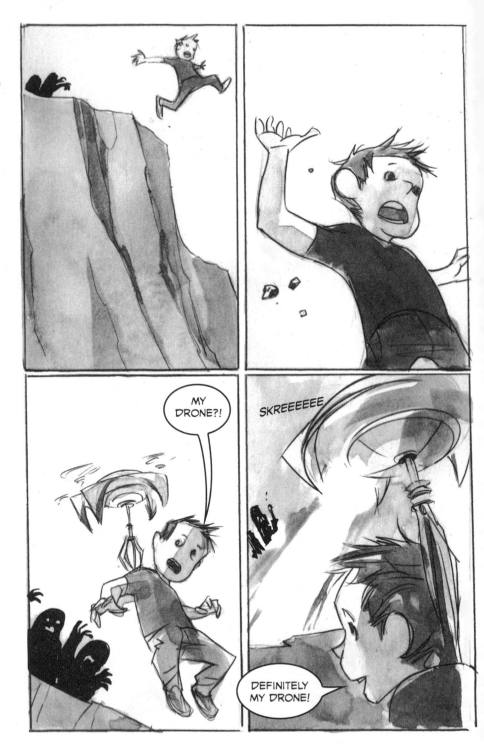

TOUCHDOWN!
SORRY FOR THE ROUGH RIDE. STILL GETTING USED TO THE CONTROLS.
YOU WERE PERFECT. THANKS!
SOMEONE WANTS TO SAY SOMETHING TO YOU.
WE'RE SOWWWWY!

WHY WOULD YOU DO IT? AFTER WE RESCUED YOU, WHY WOULD YOU STEAL FROM US?
FOR FUNSIES!
THIS PLACE IS SO DREARY, EVEN FOR YOU. IT NEEDED THE SMILES.
I REMEMBER THE SANDPIT UP AHEAD. WE'LL DROP 'EM OFF ON THE WAY OUT.
WHAAAAA?
YOU'RE RIGHT. I NEEDED THAT SMILE.

USERNAME: BWAYNE
RE: JOURNAL ENTRY 12

I'M TYPING THIS ON MY RECOVERED BATCOMPUTER. EVEN THOUGH THE JOKER AND HARLEY STOLE IT AND THE DRONE, WE WERE ABLE TO GET IT BACK. THEY'VE RUN OFF AGAIN, PRESUMABLY TO CAUSE MORE TROUBLE.

ALSO, THE DRONE IS FIXED, MEANING WE'VE BEEN ABLE TO LOCATE THE BEACON. WE CAN GO BACK TO THE ENTRANCE AND TRY TO FIND OUR WAY HOME. WE'RE ONE STEP CLOSER TO GETTING OUT OF HERE! I'M NOT LOOKING FORWARD TO RETURNING TO HOMEWORK AND AWARDS CEREMONIES. BUT I AM LOOKING FORWARD TO GETTING SAND OUT OF MY SHOES.

MAP BACK
TO ENTRY POINT

144

WE'RE NEAR THE BEACON. IT'S JUST OVER THE RIDGE ON THE OTHER SIDE.
GGRRRAAAARRRHHH!
CRUNCH
WHO OR WHAT IS THAT?
DOOMSDAY . . .
WHAT?
JUST SOMETHING I HEARD.
EVEN IF WE GOT PAST THAT . . . THING . . . WE HAVE NO IDEA HOW TO REOPEN THE DOORWAY TO GET US HOME.

ZONE DOOR AM ONE WAY
OF COURSE IT'S A ONE-WAY DOOR.
BY ACTIVATING ONLY FROM THE OUTSIDE, IT PREVENTS ANY "BAD STUDENTS" FROM BEING ABLE TO ESCAPE FROM THE INSIDE.
SO . . . WE'RE STUCK HERE. FOREVER.
OR MAYBE NOT . . .
YOU'VE GOT THAT LOOK. HE'S GOT THAT LOOK.

WHAT'S THE TIME?
I DON'T HAVE A WATCH. WHY DOES IT MATTER?
WHAT'S THE TIME? *WHAT'S THE TIME?!*
WAIT, THE DRONE HAS IT!
OUTTATHEWAY!
WHAT IS IT?
IT'S 4:00 . . . WE'RE ABOUT TO GET SOME HELP . . . AT LEAST, I HOPE.

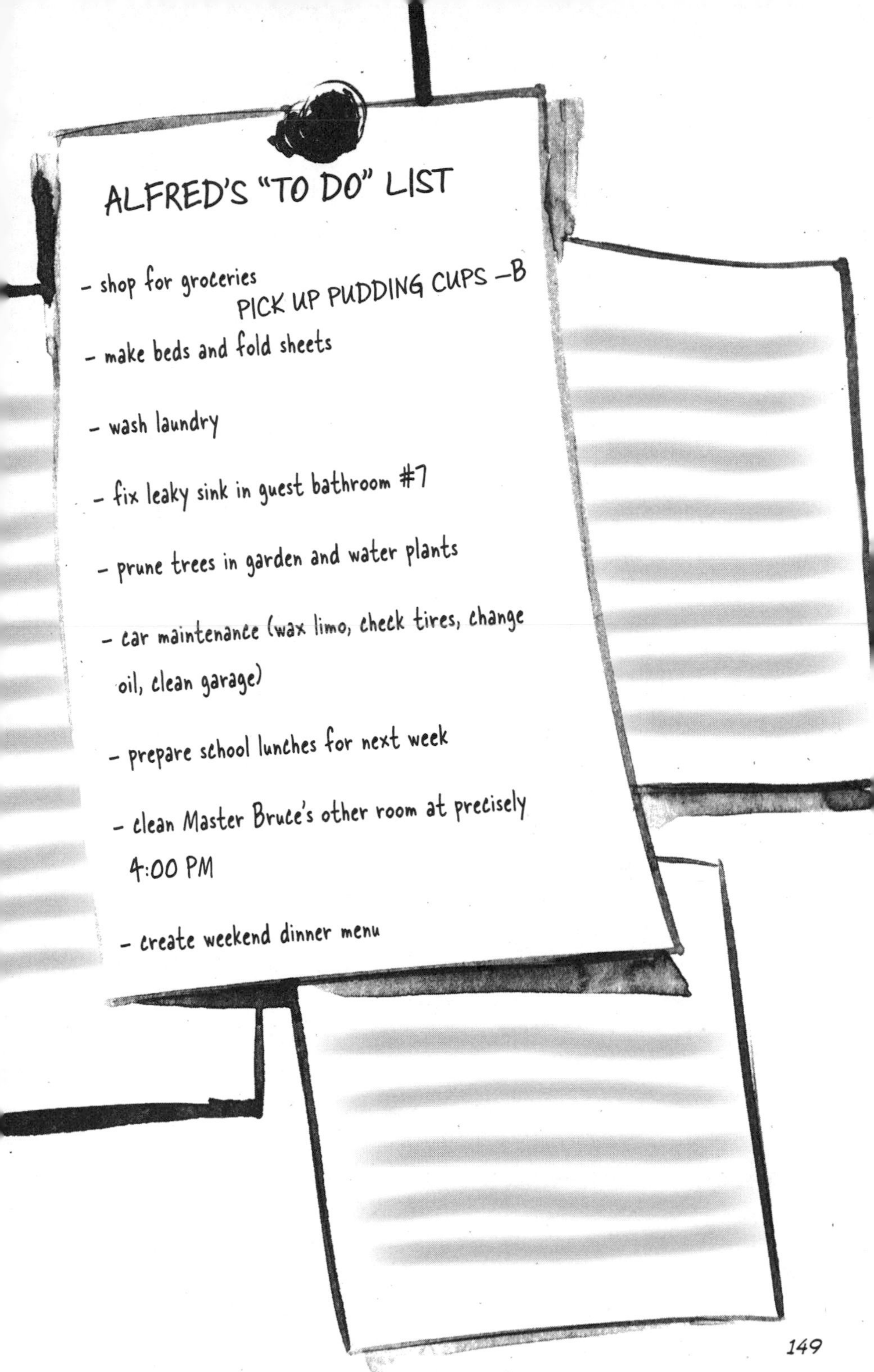

ALFRED'S "TO DO" LIST

- shop for groceries
        PICK UP PUDDING CUPS —B
- make beds and fold sheets

- wash laundry

- fix leaky sink in guest bathroom #7

- prune trees in garden and water plants

- car maintenance (wax limo, check tires, change
  oil, clean garage)

- prepare school lunches for next week

- clean Master Bruce's other room at precisely
  4:00 PM

- create weekend dinner menu

ALFRED!
I need this cleaned.
Please dust thoroughly
and hold on to something
tight.
-Bruce

FRIZZAP
HOW DID THAT HAPPEN?!
I LEFT A NOTE FOR ALFRED TO CLEAN MY TROPHY BACK HOME. BUTLERS ARE THE BEST!
WE CAN'T GET TO THE OPENING WITH HIM THERE!
WE CAN IF WE KNOCK HIM OUT OF THE WAY!
GRAHHHH!
YOU GUYS DON'T HAVE POWERS, REMEMBER?
AND THAT OPENING IS STARTING TO CLOSE. THIS IS OUR LAST CHANCE!

ENEMIES WALK LATER!

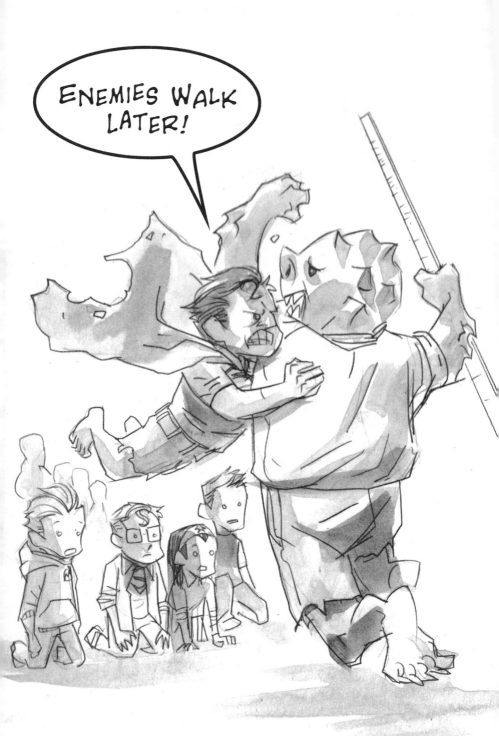

THAT'S OUR OPENING. COME ON, WE'VE GOTTA GO!
BIZARRO, COME ON! I MEAN—
YOU AM COME!
ME AM HERO
GOOD-BYE, BIZARRO!

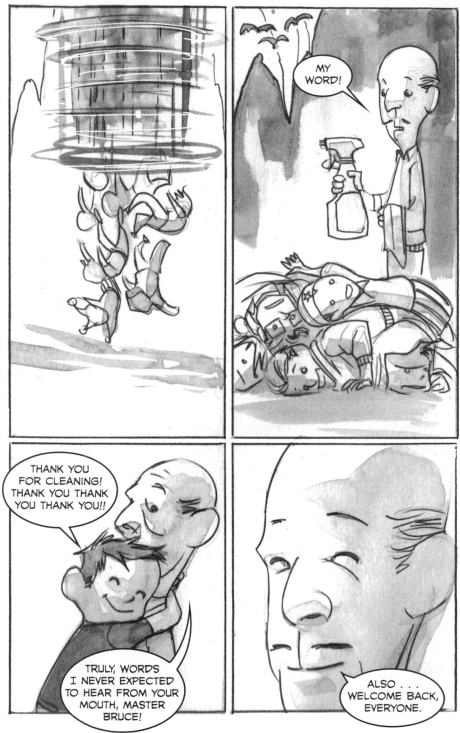

MY WORD!

THANK YOU FOR CLEANING! THANK YOU THANK YOU THANK YOU!!

TRULY, WORDS I NEVER EXPECTED TO HEAR FROM YOUR MOUTH, MASTER BRUCE!

ALSO . . . WELCOME BACK, EVERYONE.

Master Bruce,

I hope this letter finds you safe upon your return. It has been hard to keep myself busy without you around to brighten my day. No kitchen accidents to clean up. No dirty clothes to pick up after. No healthy meals to make or vegetables to force you to eat. No science experiments gone wrong or fire departments to call. Even the bats are staying quiet in the cave and not getting into the house.

Yes, without you around, things are much more quiet and peaceful.

Please return soon!!

Sincerely,

Alfred

USERNAME: BWAYNE
RE: JOURNAL ENTRY 13

WE'RE HOME!!!

I WAS SUCCESSFUL IN REMEMBERING ALFRED'S CLEANING
SCHEDULE. HIS HELP ACTIVATING THE DOORWAY INTO
THE PHANTOM DETENTION ZONE ALLOWED US TO ESCAPE.
NOT ALL OF US WERE SO LUCKY. BIZARRO WAS LEFT
BEHIND. BUT IF HE HADN'T BEEN, THEN DOOMSDAY
MIGHT'VE GOTTEN FREE TO STOP US. IT WAS A NOBLE
SACRIFICE BY A REAL HERO.

NOW THAT WE'RE BACK, WE HAVE NO TIME TO REST.
OUR SIGHTS ARE SET BACK ON LEX. HE'S THE ONE
RESPONSIBLE FOR ALL OUR PROBLEMS. AND HE'S THE
ONE WE NEED TO BRING TO JUSTICE!

BUT FIRST, SOMETHING TO EAT. ALFRED IS ALREADY
IN THE KITCHEN PREPARING OUR MEAL. HE GUARANTEES
ME IT'S NOT PIZZA, BUT MY DETECTIVE SENSE SMELLS
PEPPERONI.

PHANTOM PARTY
IN "HONOR" OF THOSE IN DETENTION

PLACE: LUTHOR TOWER
DATE: SATURDAY 9:00 PM

FOOD, DRINKS, AND ENTERTAINMENT PROVIDED

BYOBS (BRING YOUR OWN BAD SELF)
DRESS APPROPRIATELY (COSTUME COSTUME COSTUME)

RSVP - YOU AND A GUEST

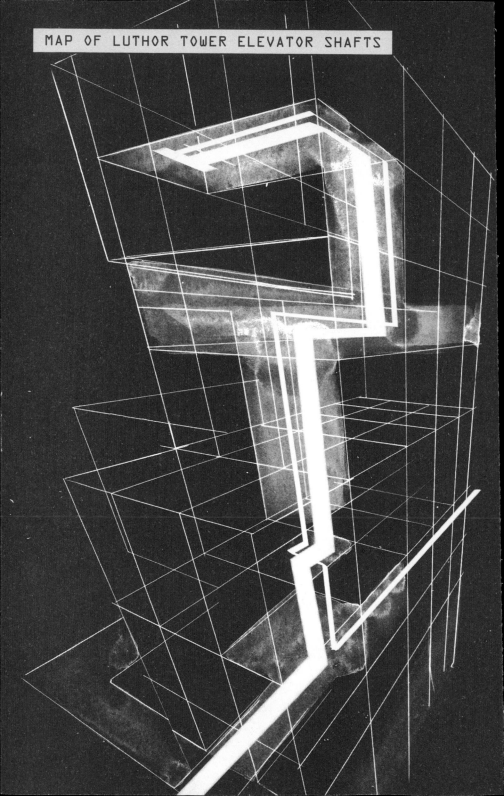

MAP OF LUTHOR TOWER ELEVATOR SHAFTS

MESSAGES

GROUP CHAT

thanks Ollie for snagging that invite

it's the perfect plan

happy to help stick it to Lex

we get inside, avoid detection, and drop off the package

hows everyone doing? check in

Here

inside but hiding in a room

I'm stuck in one of the elevators

I touched all the floor buttons out of habit

can you help us out Vic?

of course

let me see what I can do

SEND

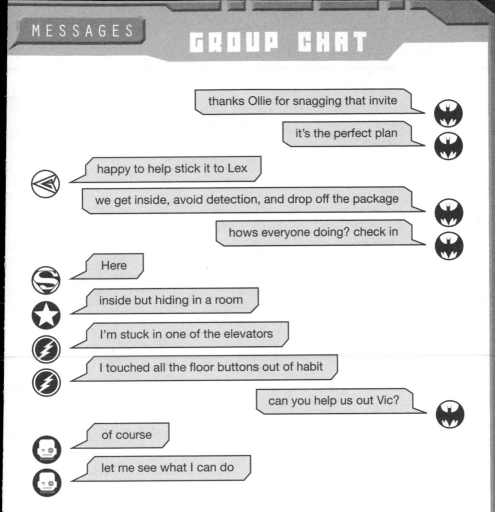

LUTHOR TOWER SECURITY ROOM
ELEVATOR
FIRE ALARM

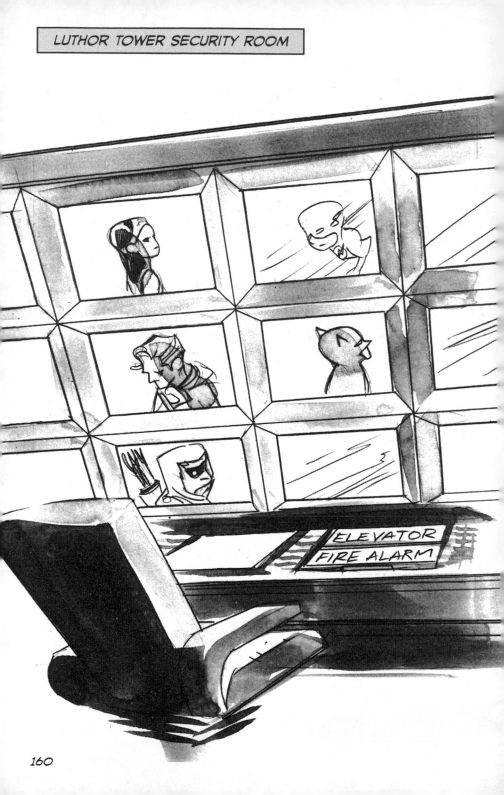

ELEVATOR
FIRE ALARM

MESSAGES

GROUP CHAT

hack went smooth

was able to provide all of you some cover or help

security cameras are on a loop and some shut down

rooms you need are unlocked

thanks Vic

you found all the alarms and shut them off?

pretty sure I spotted all of them

I'll check again

SEND

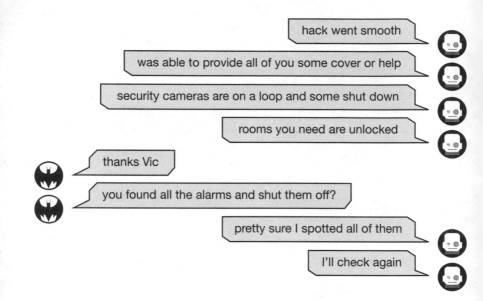

PARTY
PHOTOS

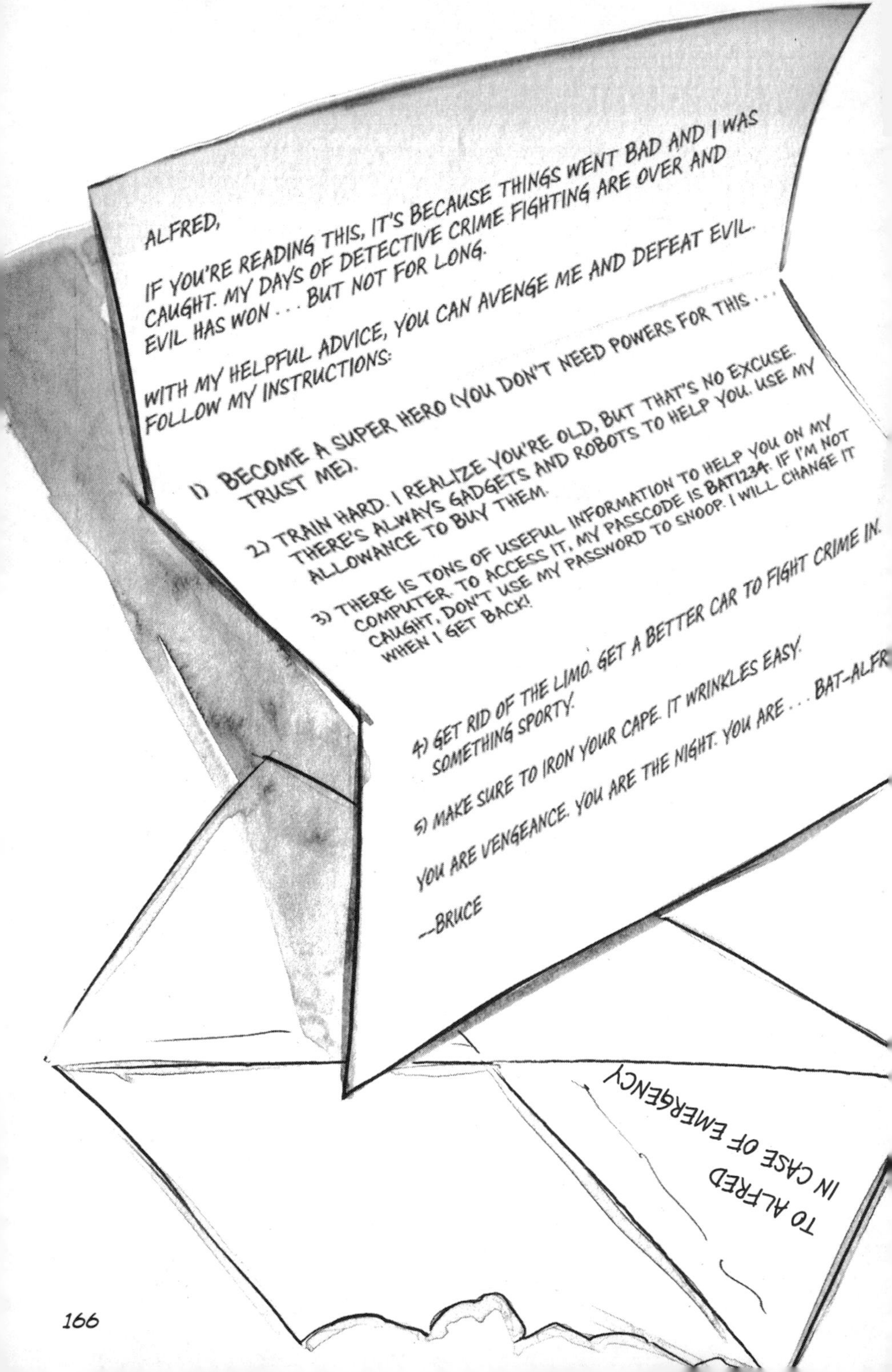

ALFRED,

IF YOU'RE READING THIS, IT'S BECAUSE THINGS WENT BAD AND I WAS
CAUGHT. MY DAYS OF DETECTIVE CRIME FIGHTING ARE OVER AND
EVIL HAS WON . . . BUT NOT FOR LONG.

WITH MY HELPFUL ADVICE, YOU CAN AVENGE ME AND DEFEAT EVIL.
FOLLOW MY INSTRUCTIONS:

1) BECOME A SUPER HERO (YOU DON'T NEED POWERS FOR THIS . . .
TRUST ME).

2) TRAIN HARD. I REALIZE YOU'RE OLD, BUT THAT'S NO EXCUSE.
THERE'S ALWAYS GADGETS AND ROBOTS TO HELP YOU. USE MY
ALLOWANCE TO BUY THEM.

3) THERE IS TONS OF USEFUL INFORMATION TO HELP YOU ON MY
COMPUTER. TO ACCESS IT, MY PASSCODE IS BAT123A. IF I'M NOT
CAUGHT, DON'T USE MY PASSWORD TO SNOOP. I WILL CHANGE IT
WHEN I GET BACK!

4) GET RID OF THE LIMO. GET A BETTER CAR TO FIGHT CRIME IN.
SOMETHING SPORTY.

5) MAKE SURE TO IRON YOUR CAPE. IT WRINKLES EASY.

YOU ARE VENGEANCE. YOU ARE THE NIGHT. YOU ARE . . . BAT-ALFR

—BRUCE

TO ALFRED
IN CASE OF EMERGENCY

KLIK
THEY'RE HERE! TAKE COVER!
THERE'S NOWHERE TO HIDE AND NO WAY OUT!
WHOOOOOOOSH
JUST PLAY ALONG.
NUDGE NUDGE
I GAVE YOU GUYS A MAKEOVER . . .

UH . . . ME AM BIZARRO?
BATZARRO.
NEVER SEEN SOMETHING THIS BIZARRE BEFORE?
THE NAME'S BIZARRA.
THE WIZARD MERLYN AT YOUR SERVICE.
AND I'M REVERSE-FLASH. I DO EVERYTHING IN REVERSE.
INSTEAD OF STEALING ONE OF YOUR GIFTS, I'VE GIVEN YOU ONE. ENJOY!

NICE TO MEET NEW FRIENDS!
RIIIIP
HMMM . . . THIS LOOKS ODDLY FAMILIAR . . .
FRIZZAP

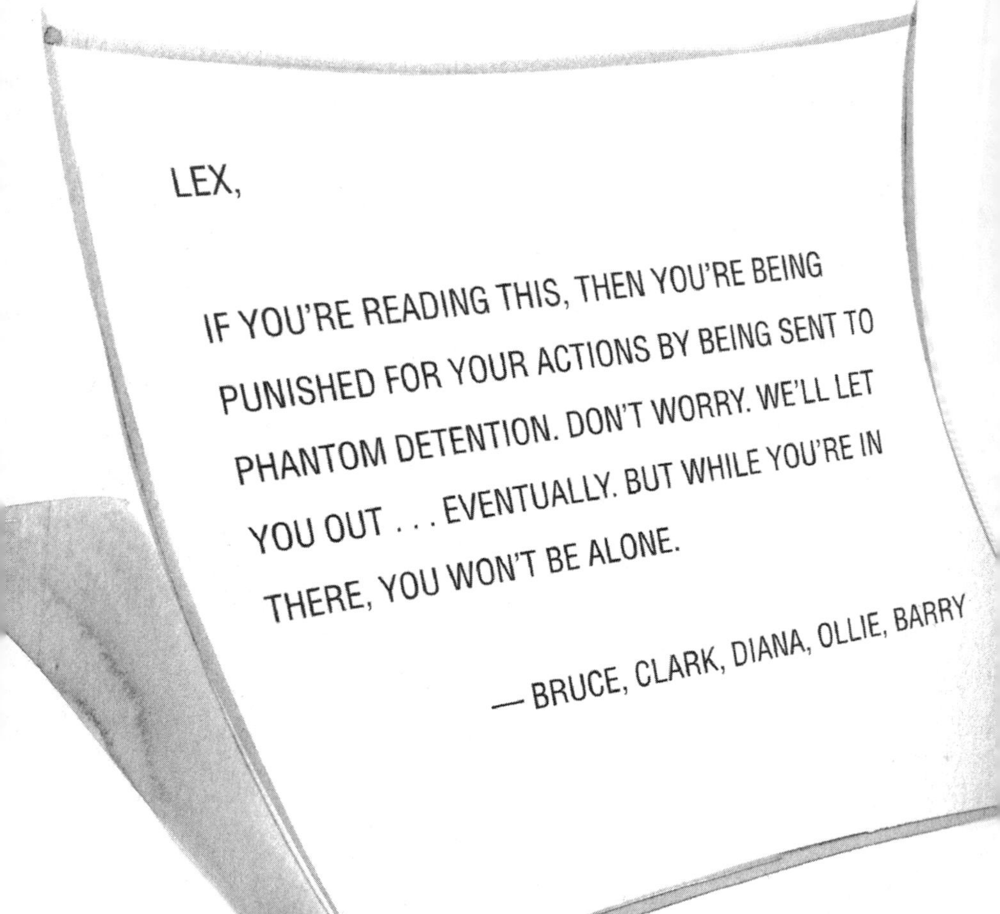

LEX,

IF YOU'RE READING THIS, THEN YOU'RE BEING PUNISHED FOR YOUR ACTIONS BY BEING SENT TO PHANTOM DETENTION. DON'T WORRY. WE'LL LET YOU OUT . . . EVENTUALLY. BUT WHILE YOU'RE IN THERE, YOU WON'T BE ALONE.

— BRUCE, CLARK, DIANA, OLLIE, BARRY

USERNAME: BWAYNE
RE: JOURNAL ENTRY 14

LEX AND HIS BULLY FRIENDS HAVE BEEN SENT TO DETENTION . . . PHANTOM DETENTION! IT WAS SO GREAT TO TURN THE TABLES ON LEX AFTER EVERYTHING HE PUT US THROUGH. I'D LOVE TO SEE THE LOOK ON HIS FACE WHEN HE REALIZES WE'RE THE ONES RESPONSIBLE. COULDN'T HAVE HAPPENED TO A WORSE GUY.

IT'S SO GOOD TO BE HOME. I HOPE I NEVER HAVE TO GO TO ANOTHER AWARDS CEREMONY FOR THE REST OF MY LIFE. IN FACT, I'D LIKE TO JUST CHANGE MY STUDIES. MAYBE I CAN ENCOURAGE ALFRED TO GET ME A PRIVATE TUTOR. MAYBE I CAN TRAVEL AROUND THE WORLD AND LEARN FROM THE BEST TEACHERS IN EVERY FIELD.

AFTER THE CRAZY ADVENTURE WE JUST HAD, WE'RE ALL EXCITED TO BE HONORING OUR OWN PERSONAL HEROES IN OUR LIVES . . .

Diana at home

Barry in school

Clark home
MARK YOUR CALENDARS
APPRECIATION DAY NOMINATIONS DUE SOON
AWARDS TO BE SPONSORED BY QUEEN INDUSTRIES

WHAT IS ALL THIS?
YOU ALWAYS WAIT ON ME. AND NOW I'D LIKE TO DO THAT FOR YOU.
THE BUTLER APPRECIATION AWARD GOES TO YOU.
SUCH A PLEASANT . . . THOUGHT. THANK YOU, MASTER BRUCE.
BESIDES . . . IT'S YOUR DAY OFF. YOU CAN GO BACK TO CLEANING THE KITCHEN TOMORROW.
MY WORD!

etention Day 1
omework forever!

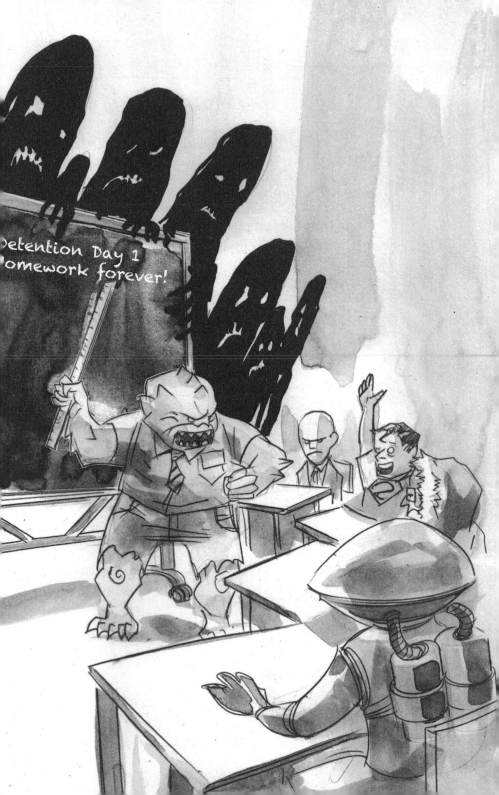

Derek Fridolfs

Derek Fridolfs is a *New York Times* bestselling writer. With Dustin Nguyen, he cowrote the Eisner-nominated *Batman: Li'l Gotham*. He's also worked on a range of titles including *Arkham City* with Paul Dini, *Adventures of Superman, Detective Comics, Sensation Comics Featuring Wonder Woman*, and comics based on Grumpy Cat and WWE pro wrestling. He's written and drawn comics based on the cartoons *Adventure Time, Regular Show, Clarence, Pig Goat Banana Cricket, Pink Panther's The Inspector, Dexter's Laboratory, Teenage Mutant Ninja Turtles, Teen Titans Go!, Looney Tunes*, and *Scooby-Doo, Where Are You!* Recently, Derek has also been fortunate to collaborate with producer/screenwriter Bob Gale to cowrite a *Back to the Future* miniseries called *Biff to the Future*.

Dustin Nguyen

Dustin Nguyen is a *New York Times* bestselling and Eisner Award–winning American comics creator. His body of work includes the co-creation of *Batman: Li'l Gotham*, numerous DC, Marvel, Dark Horse, and Boom! titles along with Image Comics' *Descender*, which he co-created. He lives in California with his wife, Nicole; their two kids, Bradley and Kaeli; and dog, Max. His first children's picture book, titled *What Is It?*, is written by his wife (at the age of 10) and is their first collaboration together. He enjoys sleeping and driving.